SPELL OR HIGH WATER

An Elemental Witches of Eternal Springs Cozy Mystery

GINA LAMANNA

LaManna Books

Copyright © 2018 by Gina LaManna

All rights reserved.

No part of this book may be reproduced in any form or by any electronic or mechanical means, including information storage and retrieval systems, without written permission from the author, except for the use of brief quotations in a book review.

❦ Created with Vellum

Acknowledgments

To the three ladies who made this project possible—Amanda, Leighann, and Annabel —thank you with all the cherries on top!

To the readers who've been following this shared world series—I hope you've been enjoying the broomstick ride across Eternal Springs.

To my husband and most favorite mechanic!

One

What a beautiful day, Paul croaked. *Paradise.*

"Quiet, Paul," I hissed through torrents of rain. Thunder cracked overhead and a bolt of lightning streaked across the scudding clouds. I gave an exhausted sigh and urged my scooter onward. "Come on, baby. Come on — you can do it!"

The motor strained, wheezed and spluttered.

I don't think it's going to make it, Paul said. *Your bike's sounding pretty gnarly there, Evian Brooks.*

"No kidding." Still, I pressed forward, praying to the storm gods to let up for a moment. Just a moment. "We're going to make it."

No, Paul said. *No, I don't think you will, Evian Brooks.*

"Just call me *Evian*!" I grunted, as a clap of thunder rattled all Eternal Springs. By the time the next lightning strike hit, my scooter had stalled and I was dripping wet and freezing, pushing the stupid vehicle up the hill.

"Thanks a lot, Paul. You jinxed me."

I'm just a toad. I can't use magic or jinxes.

"Right. Which makes me an idiot because I'm arguing

with a *toad*!" I shook my head and leaned against the scooter. I probably shouldn't take out my anger on my familiar. Paul-the-Toad is a friendly thing, albeit dry and a bit boring. He struggles to pick up on sarcasm, and he refuses to call me by anything but my full name: Evian Brooks.

See, I'm a water witch here in Eternal Springs. I've been banished to the island along with three other witches — former classmates from St. Joan of Arc — thanks to a little "incident" that blew up in my face thirteen years ago.

Paul-the-Toad is my familiar, and while he can't speak aloud, he croaks loud enough that my neighbors have complained — then again, Bertha complains about *everything*! I've been conversing with him in my head through a special little bond for as long as I can remember. And still he won't give up calling me by my full name. It can be tiring.

"I can't believe Skye is being so petty!" I shouted to the heavens. "Not today, Skye! I apologized for the wet mark on your pants."

I knew my sometimes friend, sometimes enemy couldn't hear me, but it felt good to yell. Skye Thorton, the wind witch (one of the three other protectors of Eternal Springs), must have sent a huge, squalling gust of wind across the island as a practical joke on me. Just yesterday I'd predicted on air that we'd have a bright and sunny day here on Eternal Springs. Thanks to my old pal Skye, however, the crew at the station would be laughing their heads off by the time I arrived for work.

Work is a loose term I use to call what I do. I not only own radio station Hex 66.6, but I also have a segment as a deejay, and I *love* it — with one caveat. Technology tends to go berserk here on the island, so it never quite works properly. This means the radio station rarely works for most folks, and my show reaches only a handful of people each day. It isn't all that much of a catastrophe for programs like Mitzi's

Knitting Circle (the mayor's wife's snoozefest of a segment), but it isn't working for me.

Zola's theory is that it's all the magic zipping and zapping every which way, but I'm not convinced the coven hasn't put a jinx on us just for kicks. Exhibit A: The station somehow has gotten stuck playing a bizarre twist on calypso music that everyone across the island (including myself) universally hates. At least half the population has actually thrown their devices out the window, and I suspect the other half only uses it as a tool to fall back to sleep thanks to Mitzi's interminable dreck about knitting.

Looks like you broke down, Paul said from his perch in the handlebar basket of the scooter. *Bummer.*

"Thanks, Paul." He basked in the wash of rain that'd left me annoyed and frozen straight through. I decided to attempt a quick chant and make use of the witch talents that were responsible for keeping me here in the first place: "Rain, rain, go away, come again another day! Keep me dry, so I can fly. And when I find that stupid Skye, I will poke her in the eye!"

That's not a real spell, Paul said, famously missing my sarcasm once again. *Are you sure this is Skye's fault?*

"She's upset I broke the story about the stolen beach towels before she did," I said. "There's not much happening for her to report about in Eternal Springs. Robbery is a huge deal."

It wasn't a real theft, Paul said, *someone accidentally picked them up and washed them. They were returned after a few hours, cleaner than when they'd been 'stolen.'*

"I know that, Paul." I pushed my scooter up the hill, grunting as I summited the top. "Geez, Paul, lay off the hot dogs — I can barely move this thing with you on it."

Paul croaked. He was right; the problem wasn't him, it was my stupid scooter and Skye's silly storm. I kept on pushing, hoping nobody would notice the puddle I'd leave in my chair at the office — especially not Leonard Buffet. As the owner of the radio station, I didn't *technically* have a boss to report to, but I did have Leonard, the guy I'd hired to run everything that I didn't want to do: advertising, logistics, scheduling, etc. He liked to say he ran the place. Sometimes I forgot he wasn't my boss.

The end of my struggle was in sight! Just a few more feet and I'd be able to coast down the hill and to the front door of the office. I had been running late before my scooter broke down, no thanks to Skye, the elements or a malfunctioning radio alarm. There was no time to head home for a change of clothes. At this point, powering through was the only option.

"Need a hand?"

I flicked my gaze up and found Mason Cooper jogging over, his face painted with a look of concern. I pretended not to notice the form-fitting black T-shirt that had molded to his body under the rain, or the way his jeans hugged legs that went on and on and on. We were familiar with one another, but I wouldn't call us friends by any stretch.

"He's jogging," I said to Paul. "I don't understand people who jog in the morning. Who is he, Mr. Fitness?"

He's coming to help you, Evian Brooks. Would it kill you to be nice to him?

"Yes," I snapped.

There was nothing exactly wrong with Mason Cooper, but I was uncomfortable and my pants were chafing and I didn't feel like being nice. Not to mention, I looked like a drowned rat as he jogged through the streets all handsome and successful and attractive. Mason ran the island's only mechanic shop, and I was convinced that my malfunctioning scooter alone kept him in business.

His dating resume was as long as my Christmas list (which was pretty long, seeing as I didn't find myself shopping on the mainland much) and filled with beautiful women he'd wined, dined and dumped. Or so the rumors said. It's not as if I knew firsthand, because Mason Cooper isn't my type. Not at all.

He looks nice, doesn't he? Paul offered. *You know you can't hide your thoughts from me.*

I ignored my familiar as he croaked. Then I ignored the human, too, and kept on pushing my scooter. That made for two I was ignoring this morning.

Mason looked over at him. "Is your toad okay?"

"His name's Paul, and he's fine. Just feeling sassy this morning," I said as wind whipped hair across my face. I must really look *great*. "I'm fine, Mason — get back to your jogging or whatever."

"I'm not jogging," he said. "I just came out here to help. Looks like you could use a hand — scooter acting up?"

"No, I really enjoy pushing it uphill in torrential downpours. I'm not late to work or frozen through to the bone or anything like that."

Mason's lips sealed into a thin line. "Did I do something to offend you, Evian?"

I stopped pushing the bike and faced him. I pretended I'd only stopped to have a conversation, but really I needed a breather before I continued. Either Paul needed a diet or the scooter was really quite heavy.

"You didn't do anything to me," I said. "But I saw you last night at Coconuts."

"Everyone was there. It was the kickoff for the beauty pageant contestants."

"Yeah, I know," I said, raising my eyebrows. "You made a lot of friends, seemed like."

Playboy extraordinaire Mason Cooper raised his eyebrows. "I was the emcee for the evening. I had to be nice to everyone. Look, Evian, you're not annoyed I got the emcee job for the kickoff, are you? It was just one night for laughs."

"Nope." I didn't fool myself. Of course I was annoyed! I was the only professional radio deejay on the island (again, not counting Mitzi Snoozefest), yet the beauty pageant organizers had asked Mason Cooper — local mechanic — to host Eternal Springs's biggest tourist event of the season: the beauty pageant's welcome night at Coconuts.

Women had begun arriving from destinations across the country the previous evening, and we'd celebrated the official kickoff of the pageant at the tiki bar fondly called Coconuts. There, karaoke was king and drinks were poured in glasses the size of bathtubs. It was a town ritual to be seen at Coconuts on a Friday night.

Mason folded his arms. "Look, it's not a big deal — they're not even paying me. I only said I'd do it because I didn't think anyone else wanted to."

"I'm not taking your sloppy seconds! Plus, the ladies in the pageant wouldn't be as interested in looking at me as they are ogling you."

A half smile quirked his face. "If I didn't know better, Evian Brooks, I'd say you're a little jealous."

Agreed, Paul croaked.

"Watch it or I'm having frog legs for dinner," I said to my familiar. Louder, I spoke to Mason. "In your dreams, Cooper. Now look out, please. I'm late for work."

"When should I expect your scooter at the shop?"

"Tonight!" I hollered over my shoulder. "And I need all the discounts you can give me!"

As I crested the top of the hill, his peal of laughter followed me down the other side. I almost smiled, but that would feel sacrilegious, so I kept it hidden as I sped down the hill.

The wind whipped through my hair and finally, finally, the

rain pattered to a stop as I really got momentum in my downhill coasting. I was practically flying by the time I reached the bottom. The sun had begun to peek out from behind the clouds, and I was just starting to chance a smile when *whabam!*

The crash came sudden and fast. Sand plus a slippery road combined to form an epic disaster as my scooter hit an ugly patch of slickness. I spun out, sending me, Paul and the bike careening from the road. We tottered through bushes, bulldozed a flimsy fence that needed updating and plowed straight into someone's backyard.

I leapt from the bike and reached for Paul, tucking him to my chest as the bike bumped and bounced another ten feet before finally landing across the poor, unsuspecting diving board of an in-ground pool.

Ribbet, Paul said, and he sounded ticked.

"I saved your life!" I raised my palm to meet him eye to eye, but he was uninterested in forgiving me and hopped away. "Hey! Where are you going?"

I trailed off when I saw exactly why Paul had leapt from my palm. The sparkling expanse of blue of the pool stretched before me. We'd been about a foot from ending up underwater. It would've been a nightmare to fish my scooter out of there, and because I didn't have a ton of money to replace a drowned bike I was relieved my scooter had only gone through a fence and some bushes that needed pruning anyway.

I heard Paul's panicked croak and looked up from the scooter to find him frozen on the edge of the pool.

"Will you get over here? We have to let the owner of this place know ... ." I trailed off as I joined Paul poolside and stared at a floating object. It took too long to realize that it wasn't some inflatable pool toy a kid had left out overnight — it was a body. "Oh, fudge! That's a person, Paul. A dead body!"

Paul croaked in horror. Despite feeling queasy at the sight of the woman, her hair fanning around her head in a deadly sort of halo, I chanced one more look at her face and groaned when I recognized her.

Marilyn Johnson: reigning Eternal Springs Beauty Pageant queen.

It appeared Marilyn's time to rule had come to an end. The only place she'd be getting a makeover from here on out was the morgue.

Two

"Yep, she's dead," the medical examiner said. "Definitely dead."

"No kidding," I mumbled. "What tipped you off? The strangulation marks around her neck or the fact there's no breathing or heartbeat?"

"Strangulation marks?" Dr. Abigail Marley glanced at me and tried to frown. But her Botox was just too much, and she couldn't quite force her face into the emotion. "Oh, gee — look at that. She was strangled!"

"I think the bigger question is whether she was strangled before or after she was pushed into the pool," I said, guiding Abigail along. "You'll have to determine the time and cause of death."

"Yes, I suppose."

Abigail wasn't exactly a medical genius — unless you counted her work as a plastic surgeon. Eternal Springs is a small island, so we make do with what we have. When she wasn't injecting Botox at the spa, Abigail served as a quasi-medical examiner.

"How'd you get here so fast?" I asked her. "I didn't even have a chance to call for help before you popped up."

"I heard you scream," she said quickly, leaving me to wonder if I'd screamed and forgotten about it. I didn't remember screaming. "Anyway, we need to get the police here. I'm sure the mayor will be along. It's not every day we have a disaster of this magnitude."

Disaster would be a good word to describe the situation. Unbeknownst to me, I'd stumbled across the semi-private hideaway that housed the girls registered to compete in the pageant. The Beauty Cottage, they'd called it. A big house, complete with a stunning view of the beach, a plethora of rooms and bunk beds inside, and a huge pool outside that would probably never be used again.

One or two of the girls, having heard the commotion, peeped from the windows. One brave soul ventured out. I squinted but didn't recognize this one. I'd met many of the C-list contestants last night at Coconuts, where I'd been slumming, trying to convince a few of the A-listers to appear on my radio show for interviews and to drum up additional excitement for the week's festivities.

I'd settled on a few B-listers because Tarryn and Marilyn — the two women thought to vie for the prestigious first-place crown — had declined to comment. I now felt bad about my annoyance at Mary, seeing as she wouldn't be giving interviews ever again.

"Marilyn Johnson," the medical examiner said, squatting near the body. She sounded just a little too gleeful saying the victim's name. "Not so beautiful now, is she?"

"Abigail!" I gasped. "That's horrible to say. She just died!"

"Died?" One of the pageant girls said. "Who's dead? I thought Mary was just doing some weird beauty ritual floating there."

"Idiot," Abigail murmured. Then she announced: "Marilyn's dead. Someone call the police."

The pageant contestant paused, her lip quivering. "But —."

"The police!" I shouted. "Call the police from the landline. Cellphones don't work all that well out here."

Instead of reacting in a calm and logical manner, the girl crumpled to her knees and began to scream. This drew another girl to her side, and then another, and one by one, the house emptied of girls as they flocked poolside to sob and hug each other.

"Where'd you say you came from again?" I asked Abigail. "How did you beat the police here? I *just* fell through the fence."

"I think we need to get started investigating," she said, ignoring my question. "Let's see, I think I have a camera here somewhere to snap a few photos."

I was pulled from my line of questioning when I felt a hand on my shoulder and jumped. "Mason!"

"What's going on here?" His good-natured grin had been replaced by a stern expression. "I heard screaming."

"Yeah, well, we uncovered a body," I said. "Marilyn Johnson. Do you know her?"

Mason's face went pale. I took that to mean she'd been on his Christmas-list roster of ex-girlfriends.

"Mason," I snapped. "Get a handle on yourself and go call the police. I have to make sure Abigail doesn't contaminate the crime scene any more than she already has."

I gestured to the medical examiner. She'd reached for Mary's shoe, latched on, and began half-heartedly pulling the body toward her until I'd instructed her to stop.

Mason gave a firm nod and, unlike everyone else who'd joined the crime scene, didn't collapse into a fit of tears and fanning and makeup-application in case the media appeared to report on the crime scene.

I rolled my eyes, thinking that the media would be none other than Skye Thorton, the only reporter for The Town Croaker — our local paper. If it weren't for Skye I wouldn't be here in the first place. I'd be at work getting warm, starting my broadcast and ... *crap*! Work!

With a wash of relief, I realized that things hadn't worked out so badly for me. They sure had for poor Mary Johnson, but the folks at the station surely would understand my tardiness once I explained. If anything, it was a blessing in disguise I'd discovered the body. I'd been able to get the police called faster *and* I wouldn't have to make up a lame excuse about what had held me up.

I took it upon myself to usher the girls back from the edge of the pool, sequestering them in a flighty knot of dressing gowns and nude shades of lipstick. Most of them turned their back on the pool and launched into a twitter of gossip over who might have wanted Mary dead. Rumors flew, and I tried to listen in, at least until our next guest arrived.

"What happened?" Barnaby Sterling Montgomery, the town mayor, pulled up on his golf cart. He was wildly lazy and preferred to drive around the island instead of walking the short distances everywhere. His wife, Mitzi, was as usual knitting away next to her husband with an angry *click-click-click*. "Oh my, a murder at the Beauty Cottage. The *drama*!"

The mayor had proudly nicknamed himself Buddy and insisted everyone call him that instead of the horrendously long name his mother had given him. Buddy looked keenly around, struggling to pull his eyes from the gaggle of girls clad in flimsy dressing gowns with straps of lace lingerie peeking out at the shoulders and neckline when the satin fabric slipped. Meanwhile, his wife *click-click-clicked* faster, as if hoping to knit each of the girls a nice, fluffy warm coat fit for Antarctica.

"Evian found Mary Johnson face down in the pool," the medical examiner said, sounding oddly excited. "She's totally dead."

"As opposed to a little dead?" I looked at Abigail, horrified as usual that we entrusted her with such an important job.

"Yes, mayor — ."

"Buddy!" He patted his hefty stomach. "Call me Buddy, Evian. We're all friends here."

"Buddy," I gritted out. "I found Mary when I lost control of my scooter and crashed through there." I raised my hand and pointed out the path of destruction. "Paul was the only person — er, toad — with me."

"Mary." Buddy frowned, his thick cheeks turning red. "Wasn't everyone betting on her to win the contest? Not that I'm a betting man, but if I were, isn't that who I'd *theoretically* have put my money on to win?"

Abigail gave a sour nod. "She's won fifty-nine beauty pageants across the country. She was supposed to make this her sixtieth."

"Well, *that's* not happening," I said, my mind already clicking in search of foul play. I didn't know for a fact that she'd been murdered, but to my untrained eye it looked as though the red marks around her neck signaled someone's hands had recently squeezed there. "Poor thing."

"Maybe one of the other girls killed her," Abigail suggested. "Tarryn is basically a shoo-in now for first place."

I didn't like agreeing with Abigail as a general rule, but I couldn't help admitting that she had a point. It'd been exactly what I was thinking but was afraid to say. At that moment, Eternal Springs's cops arrived and took control of the scene.

Like the mayor, the police seemed to have a tough time keeping their tongues from flopping out of their mouths at the sight of so many half-dressed ladies standing around the pool.

"Gentleman," I said with a cough. "The dead body?"

Mason gave a reluctant smile at my left, having returned to my side after calling the police. He, too, looked unamused at what my dysfunctional scooter had uncovered.

"Right, right," Buddy cleared his throat importantly. "Let's get to work, ladies and gents. Anyone take photos of the scene yet?"

Abigail nodded. "And look there. We've got signs of strangulation around her neck."

One of the cops scratched his head. "We might be dealing with a murder."

I rolled my eyes. Like everything, apparently even murder investigations run on the notoriously slow island clock. "Look, I know I found the body, but I'm really late for work and the show is going to have to start with or without me. Can I give my statement and take off? You know where to find me for any follow-up questions."

The cops looked at each other, and the larger one shrugged. "Sure," he said, pulling out a notepad. "Detail your morning for me, Miss Brooks."

I reviewed my morning, focusing on the stretch of time between my scooter crapping out and my discovery of Mary's body. I glanced over to Mason for verification as I detailed our chat, and he nodded along for corroboration.

"What about before your scooter, ah, *crapped out*?" The cop asked, quoting me. "Do you have anyone to verify your whereabouts?"

"Sure — my toad, Paul," I said with an eye roll and a nod toward my shoulder, where Paul perched. "But he's a toad and doesn't talk."

"The way I see things," the cop said, "you could have come down here and killed Mary, and then gone back up the hill to get your scooter. Mason sees you, so you make up some excuse about your scooter not working, and —."

"I'm sorry for interrupting, but that makes no sense." I pointed to the scooter in the corner. "It's over there. Check it if you want. Also, what incentive do I have to kill Mary? I didn't even know the woman."

"You were talking to all the ladies last night," the cop said. "You didn't meet her?"

"Fine, I met her last night," I clarified. "But only for a second. I asked if she'd come down to the station for a quick interview sometime this week to promote the pageant."

"What'd she say?"

I shifted uncomfortably from one foot to the next. "Like many contestants, she declined."

The cop nodded, looking as though he'd cracked a difficult code. "She turned you down."

"Yes, like many of the other women —."

"You were upset with her."

"No! I wasn't upset. I mean, just a tiny bit of annoyance maybe, but not enough to kill her! I could have had an interview lined up every day by the end of the night. In fact, I have one about to start now. The contestant is probably already at the station. I have to get going ... can I leave now?"

The cops glanced at one another.

"You know where to find her," Mason said, giving them a buddy-buddy sort of look that only dudes can master. "Let her do her broadcast for the two people who listen to the show."

"I have more than two people who listen to my show!" I retorted, but I didn't mention the third person was my mother, and she rarely listened live. She still made me send her cassette tapes each week, which was another issue entirely. "But yes, anyway, Mason's right. If you have more questions I'll come down to the police station later."

"Fine, but don't leave town," one of the cops said.

I couldn't tell if he was joking, but it wasn't funny.

As if, I thought, turning to stare at my scooter in despair. I couldn't leave if I wanted. As one of four sworn protectors of the island — and not by choice — I was stuck here until there were no threats left to Eternal Springs. When might that be? Who knew? I could be stuck here forever, listening to Buddy give himself awards at every town hall meeting.

"I'll take care of the scooter," Mason said. "You can head to work."

"Really?" I hated to ask a favor of him, but the gratefulness oozed out despite my trying to maintain control. "I would really appreciate that. And listen, I'm sorry about ... before. I had a rough morning."

"We all did," he said with a dry smile. "I'll catch you later."

I nodded, thanked him again, and double-checked Paul's grip on my shoulder before I headed off to the station. I thought maybe I'd left a spare pair of jeans and a sweatshirt in my desk drawer in case of an emergency, and I prayed they were still there — and that they didn't smell.

I was an hour late. Leonard Buffet met me the second I careened into the building. His moustache — a gray, stiff caterpillar above his lip — didn't look very happy with me.

"More than an hour late! Miley is waiting for you in there. Your listeners are waiting out there." He pointed a finger outside. "They've been listening to that stupid calypso music for an hour while you've been what? Bathing in the ocean?"

"It's raining," I said, glancing down at my sopping clothes. "Or it was. And I lost control of my bike and, oh ... why am I explaining all this? First, I own this place, Leonard. Second, I found a dead body this morning."

"A dead body? What are you talking about?" He scoffed. "The deadliest thing on this island is Abigail's perfume. She can take a room out with one spritz of that stuff."

"Unfortunately, she was there too. At the crime scene as the medical examiner," I explained. "I think we have a murder on our hands."

His eyes brightened. "Nothing like a murder to boost ratings."

"That's horrible," I said, though a similar thought had crossed my mind. The difference between us is that I pushed it away out of respect for the dead. "Poor Mary is lying there in the pool, and all you can think about is ratings?"

"Mary Johnson?" His voice turned almost as gleeful as Abigail's. "She was scheduled to win this pageant! Talk about ratings. You get on this case, Evian Brooks — you hear me? I want to know the ins and outs of it before Skye gets ahold of this one."

"That's a horrible idea."

Leonard waved a hand. "Yeah, yeah. I know you feel bad and all of that jazz. Misery and sadness and funerals, yada yada." He must have seen my un-bemused expression because Leonard stopped talking and reframed his expression to one of remorse. "I know it's sad. This is my coping mechanism."

"Well, you should do a better job of being sympathetic," I said. "You sound creepy and very rude."

"I'm sorry. Look, I know this must be upsetting to you, but don't you want to help Mary?"

"I think it's too late to help her. She's dead — that's the point of my story."

"Yes, but if she was murdered we need to find justice for her. I don't know about you, but I'm not willing to put all my hopes for Mary's justice into the hands of Abigail, Buddy and the rent-a-cops we've got running this place."

"Fine, but what can I do?"

"You've always wanted to do a more investigative reporting-type show," Leonard said. "Well? This is your chance. Dig around, ask some questions, see what you can find. You'll be helping Mary, and you just might solve a murder investigation. Plus, our ratings are horrible. I can't understand why technology is such an issue on the island, but I've received seven death threats just this morning claiming people will murder me if I don't cut the calypso music. But I can't! I don't know where the heck it's coming from!"

"Don't worry," I reassured him. "I'll look into it. We'll get the ratings up."

"You'd better," he said, "or I'll be the next dead body around here, and you'll be short one excellent employee."

Three

Kenna Brynne sizzled with frustration. I should've known I'd get a visit from her. I just hadn't expected it to be on my walk of shame from the show.

My interview with beauty contestant Connie Hart had flopped. She seemed to be still drunk from karaoke the night before and slurred her way through every answer, stopping to ask for a Bloody Mary in the middle of her introduction — hugely inappropriate, considering the dead body in the pool just hours earlier.

To stall, Leonard had blasted more calypso music and we'd added three more death threats to the morning tally. It was a disaster. Plus, my underwear was still wet from the rain making me *very* uncomfortable.

I was in the middle of walking home to shower and change, muttering nonsensical curses about Connie Hart to Paul as I climbed the hill. Kenna blindsided me as I passed the Beauty Cottage.

"What were you thinking, Evian?" she snapped. "You've ruined everything. Everything!"

"Um, sorry?" I faced her, ignoring Paul's warnings to stay calm. "Do you feel like reminding me about what I did this time?"

Kenna and Skye, along with me, are three of the four witches tasked with guarding Eternal Springs from threats of the supernatural variety. Thanks to an incident when we'd studied at St. Joan of Arc — an incident that wasn't my fault, should anyone ask — we'd been deemed negligent while on watch one evening, which made it our duty to stick around and guard the portal to make sure no creatures escaped into this world. It was the definition of a thankless job.

That was the same night our school had burned down, the coven had gone fleeing to the mainland, and a heard of cats (witchy familiars who hadn't wanted to move to New Jersey) had escaped into the Cottonmouth Copse. Unfortunately, we'd been stuck here to clean up the mess and keep monsters from escaping the dreaded hole that'd been left open.

"Seriously, Evian?" Kenna tapped a pen against her ever-present clipboard. "Take a look."

I followed her line of sight to the marks left from where my scooter had skidded off the road, past the crumpled bushes and mutilated fence, into the gaping hole that had been roped off by crime scene tape.

"*Oops*," I said, turning back. "I'm sorry about the damage, but it wasn't my fault. I mean, I'll pay for it, but ... ."

"It's not about the damage!" she barked. "I'm talking about the murder!"

"Well, I definitely didn't do that. You can't believe that I'm a suspect. You know me better than just about anyone else on this island and yeah, I know that's depressing."

"I'm not talking about the murder suspect ... ." She blinked up at me. "Did you say you're a suspect?"

"Why don't I shut up and let you talk?"

Kenna shook her red hair and I swear licks of flame

singed the tips. She was truly angry. "I'm talking about the tourism industry! As you know, I head the tourism board. This beauty pageant was supposed to bring in a ton of visitors!"

"Right. I think the visitors are still here."

"You're supposed to draw people to Eternal Springs — not kill them!"

"I already told you I had nothing to do with it! I can't help that I stumbled onto the body. If it wasn't me, it would have been someone else. Whoever killed Mary, if it is in fact a murder, wasn't going to stop because the head of the tourism board asked politely."

"Well, they should." She harrumphed. "Now all the attention will be focused on her death and the media we'll get will be annoyingly negative. Here we are, supposedly drawing beautiful women to the island, and now we're killing them off."

"There's no evidence to support anyone else is getting killed off. Plus, they always say there's no such thing as bad press." I pointed toward the pool. "Not to mention, have you considered the tragedy this is for Mary and her family? I can't believe you're even thinking of the tourism board right now."

"This island's got to stay alive somehow. If we don't have visitors, we don't have a community."

"Would that be so bad?" I frowned. "Maybe if everyone left the island we wouldn't be stuck here together guarding the stupid portal."

"How dare you bring that up? Especially when it was your fault —."

"It was not my fault, Kenna. Now, my clothes are chafing in areas that aren't polite to adjust in public, so I'm going to go home to change. If you want to keep yelling at me, then you'll have to walk beside me."

"Where are you in a hurry to go?"

"Home. I told you."

"You've got that determined look in your eye, Evian. You're not fooling me."

"Fine." I wheeled to face her and Paul gave a groan of disapproval. "I'm going to ask around about Mary's death. We all know the ME isn't exactly top notch, and our police force is just too small to handle everything. I'm going to do a little investigation on my own time."

She gasped. "You're going to compete with Skye for the story."

"I'm not competing! I'm just doing my job. It might help with ratings for the show."

"You're as bad as me, you know," Kenna said, scurrying to keep up as I launched back into a march toward home, "using the murder for your own benefit."

"I'm not worried about tourism; I'm trying to get justice for Mary."

"Fine!" Kenna stopped, gasping for air as I trekked on ahead. "Run away from me, but don't you dare let this affect my numbers! Otherwise I will curse you! I will set your hair on fire!"

"I'm a water witch," I hollered back, relieved that nobody else was around to hear. Otherwise, they'd think we were crazier than they already did. "I'll hose you down, Kenna."

You have got to cool it with those girls, Paul said as I made it home and unlocked the door. *It's the four of you in this together*.

"Yeah, but not by choice," I said. "I can't believe the four of us got stuck in this mess."

Forget about that. Where are you going first?

I shrugged, which had the awkward side effect of sending Paul flying from my shoulder. He landed inches from a cup of cold coffee and shot me a haughty, disgruntled stare.

"Back to Abigail," I said. "I've been thinking about this morning, and I just can't quite figure out how she got to the crime scene so quickly. It's weird, isn't it? She avoided every question I asked."

I'm staying home. This morning was exhausting.

"You didn't even have to move anywhere!" I said. "How can you be tired?"

I want a bon bon. Paul said. *Bon bon, please.*

I sighed, forked out a bon bon and put it on the little green plate that Paul loved. It had a photo of Kermit on it. Then I headed to the shower, rinsed off and finally felt warm again.

By the time Paul had finished his bon bon (prissy little toad), I was ready to launch a murder investigation.

Four

You have to do something about the garden, Paul said. *It's no place for a toad to live.*

"It's fine!" I was on my way out the door to track down the medical examiner. Though I doubted I'd learn much from Abigail, I needed to find out if she or the police had uncovered additional details from the crime scene. "You hate being outside, anyway. You're an indoor toad."

But all my friends have started moving away. Paul sounded melancholy. *All your plants are dying.*

I stopped on the front walkway to my home and studied the lawn. "Huh," I told Paul. "Maybe you're right."

Look at your daisies. Dead as doornails. What about your ferns? It's as if they're turning to sludge.

I hesitated to kneel because I'd just showered, but I bent closer to the ground and studied the rows upon rows I'd carefully planted earlier in the year. Sure enough, at least half of the plants were dead. Some of them had even morphed into a weird sort of mush that resembled dirt but smelled like the inside of a well-used garbage can.

I waved a hand in front of my face to disperse the odor.

"Why does this always happen to me? I read the manuals. I water my plants. I put some of them in part shade and the rest in full sun as the tutorials described. I even tried to get some functioning internet to research these things!"

If you talked to Zola, maybe she could help, Paul suggested. *She doesn't have to be an enemy, you know.*

"Zola won't help me. She still thinks I'm at fault for the incident."

Everyone thinks it's everyone else's fault, Paul said, sounding as snappish as he ever got. *Why can't you girls just shoulder the blame equally and start over? You're all stuck here together. Why not make the most of it?*

"You just want your toad friends back."

That too. Conversation with you can be tedious.

"I'm the one talking to a toad!" I stood, stretched my creaky joints and realized that I wasn't as young as I used to be. Neither was Zola for that matter, and maybe Paul had a point. Maybe we could move past the stupid school nastiness and become real friends, not just pseudo friends who watched each other's backs when the going got rough. "I'm going to ask Zola for gardening help."

Good on you. Now, can you drop me off on the front steps? I don't want to get my feet dirty.

"You're the weirdest toad I know."

Kiss me, and maybe I'll turn into your prince.

"Get out of here," I said, but I gently walked him to the front and set him down. "I'll be back after my meeting with Abigail."

Is it a meeting if she doesn't know you're coming?

"Fair enough. My ambush of Abigail." I took one more glance around and studied the yard I hadn't noticed was melting before my eyes. With a grim set to my lips, I muttered, "And I'd better be ready to suck up to Zola, because she won't help me for free."

That's the spirit!

The hunt for the medical examiner was short lived. Abigail valued beauty above all things. Therefore, she spent most of her waking hours at one branch or another of Eternal Springs's spa and resort.

I entered the spa and checked in at the front desk, asking for Abigail. The receptionist pointed the way to the mud pits, so I headed in that direction, wondering why rich people paid good money to have themselves slathered in gunk. Even Paul hated to get dirty, and he's a toad.

Abigail sat in a vat of the stuff with the black mess slathered over her face, her shoulders and her lady bits, though it didn't cover all that much. I'd found her in the female-only portion of the spa, and as it turned out, ladies walked around here wearing nothing but dirt.

"Sorry to bother you," I said, crouching next to the hot tub-like pit filled with black goo that resembled the current state of my garden, just slightly less toxic-scented. "But I have a few questions for you."

Abigail's eyes flashed open, startling white against the darkness of the mud. "You're interrupting my mud bath!"

"How is this a bath? You're getting dirtier!" I shook my head. "Never mind. I will stop bothering you in just a second after I ask you a few questions."

"First Skye, then you?"

"Skye already beat me to it?"

Abigail rolled her eyes then closed them. "It's Skye's job to investigate. It's the only thing keeping her sane — otherwise she'd be forced to write about face creams and nail polishes, and we all know that would drive her into a looney bin."

I cocked my head in silent agreement. In that way, Skye and I were similar. I wanted a big radio show broadcasting important news and accurate weather and funny banter, and Skye wanted a popular column with noteworthy stories and poignant pieces. Neither of us would ever be able to achieve that so long as we were stuck in Eternal Springs, but we'd both decided to give it our best shot.

"Did you find out anything about Mary? Can you confirm if she was murdered?"

"Why should I tell you?" Abigail snarked. "I'm in a mud bath. You're interrupting my private time."

"I'll buy you a facial," I told her. "I have some credits that I won from karaoke night that are going to expire. I'll transfer them all to you."

"How many points?" When I told her the number, her eyes widened and her jaw dropped. "Okay, then sure. I can confirm Mary is dead and that she was killed."

"I'll need more than that for a hundred and two points," I said. "How? Why? Any suspects?"

"Besides yourself?"

"Me? I cannot actually be a suspect."

She shrugged. "You're as good as any. Nobody has any clue who murdered Mary, or how or why."

"I thought you said she was strangled."

"I didn't say that, but it's true," she said. "I guess we're still just lost when it comes to the who and why."

"Was she dead before she fell into the pool?"

Abigail opened one eye at me and sighed. "Here's what I have: Someone approached the victim and strangled her — a personal crime, so possibly one of passion or of anger, or both. The person also had to be strong enough to hold Mary down — it looks as though she might have fought back based on a quick glance under her fingernails, but I'll need the lab reports to confirm."

"Mary was tiny," I said. "What was she, eighty pounds soaking wet?"

"Just over one-hundred pounds and slightly more than five

feet tall. She was small," Abigail admitted. "But it's instinct to fight for your life. She would have struggled."

"Time of death?"

"You really are incessant with your questions, aren't you?" She heaved a sigh. "She wasn't dead all that long before you found her. Again, without the lab reports I can only guess. I'd put her time of death around eight that morning — just less than an hour before you found her. I believe she was dead or close to it by the time her body hit the pool, though I have some tests running that will let me know if she inhaled water. That would indicate she'd still been breathing when she hit the pool."

"She could have hit it and been unconscious but breathing," I said, "and then the official cause of death would be drowning, right?"

"For your purposes, the important fact is that someone wanted her dead." Abigail's eyes flashed open, looking eerily cold at me. "I don't think that's being questioned. The official cause of death will be but a trivial detail."

"Not trivial, but —."

"A shame she won't be able to compete in the contest, don't you think?" Abigail's face took on an odd little grin that could only be described as bizarre. "Unfortunate, really. She'd worked so hard to have sixty wins, just to fall one short ... ."

"Why are you smiling?"

"It's how I process grief," she said, giving a shake of her head. "Plus, I'm thinking of all the good Mary has done — bringing so much beauty into the world."

Abigail was starting to creep me out. I had all I needed from her for the time being, so I stood up.

Before I left, I tossed one more question over my shoulder that'd been bugging me since the morning. "Where were you this morning around eight?"

Abigail sat up, a twist of revulsion on her lips. "Are you

asking me for an alibi after I just volunteered a boatload of help to you?"

"It wasn't free help," I pointed out. "You wanted a facial."

"B-but still!" She spluttered on a hunk of mud that had dripped onto her lip. When she finally washed it away, she had streaks across her face that made the woman downright terrifying. "I will not answer that. It's an insult to me and my profession."

"You're a plastic surgeon," I said, "not an ME by training. Also, you showed up at the crime scene super-fast — a little too fast, in my opinion."

"So did you!"

"I skidded out of control and landed there! I would never have stumbled on the body otherwise."

"I had business in the area." Abigail tilted her nose high. She looked like the witch in this scenario with all the lumps and bumps caked on her skin. "And that's all you need to know, so get out of my mud bath. And transfer your points to me, you witch!"

As I turned back to reception, I hid a smile.

If only she knew the half of it.

Five

It wasn't my first choice to return to the scene of the crime, but the truth was that most people who'd known Mary had been staying with her. Marilyn, along with most of the contestants, weren't from the island. They'd traveled here for the show.

I knocked on the front door of the Beauty Cottage and was let in by Billie Jo, the only local contestant who'd made the cut.

"Hi there, Evian," she sniffed, her eyes red. "What can I do for you?"

"I'm really sorry for your loss, Billie Jo, but can I speak to a few of the girls? I've been asked to help look into Marilyn's murder."

"Oh, Mary," she gushed, a new wave of tears welling up in her eyes. "The poor thing! How tragic. And just think, it could have been any of us!"

I had considered the same thing when Abigail had told me the time of death. If I hadn't been running late to work, if I'd left an hour earlier as I'd planned in order to grab breakfast if any number of reasons had drawn me out of the house just an hour earlier, I might have stumbled upon a murder taking place. And if I had, would the killer have gotten rid of me too? Disposed of the evidence? I shuddered, thankful I'd never have to know.

"Sure, come on in. Skye just left, so the girls are still gathered," Billie Jo said. "You might as well talk to some of us now since we're all sobbing messes anyway. Some beauty contestants, huh?"

"Hey, it's okay." I pulled her in for a hug. "You guys lost a dear friend. Nobody is looking at your makeup during this time."

"Well ... ." Billie Jo led me into some sort of central living room that likely served as gossip central. "Here they are."

I understood her hesitation. About half of the girls perched on couches, chairs, chaise lounges or at the dining room table, with a compact pushed up to their noses as they reapplied makeup. The other half lounged more somberly, foregoing their faces for a more real-looking state of depression.

"Hi, I'm Evian."

"You're the girl who was trying to get us all to go on the radio at Coconuts last night, weren't you?" one of the women asked. "Wasn't your name, like, ... a water bottle or something?"

"Evian Brooks," I said with a firm smile planted on my face. "And you're right. I'm doing an investigative piece for Hex 66.6 and —."

"Just like Skye?" the same girl interrupted. "You guys have weird names. What happened to Jane and Mary and ... ." She stopped dead at the last name. "Oh, poor Mary!"

I cleared my throat. "Skye's a newspaper reporter. We're working independently. Anyway, the reason I'm here is because I'd like to ask each of you a few questions."

"Ugh, again?" the interrupter rolled her eyes. "Who knew Mary's death would be such a hassle?"

I turned to her. "Great. Let's start with you — what's your name?"

"I'm Lauren," she said. "And fine. Let's go sit on the porch so I can tan while we talk."

I followed the beauty contestant to the back of the house. When she reached the porch, she let her robe drop to reveal a slinky string bikini and plopped herself onto a lounger.

"I didn't see anything," she said, closing her eyes. "I was upstairs doing my manicure — see here, look. Pretty, isn't it?"

I studied her sparkle-tipped hand and had to turn away to prevent my eyes from getting singed at the glare. "Gorgeous. Did you hear anything?"

"Nope." She chomped on gum that she must have been storing in her cheek like a chipmunk. "I was in the bathroom with the door locked. See, it's a tricky situation here. We've got eighteen ladies and two bathrooms. You do the math. I've seen Chelsea wake up at four in the morning just to get a turn to shave her legs."

I winced. "Yikes."

"Yeah. We live in real close quarters. Then again, most of us have run into each other at other competitions, so it's not like we're total strangers."

"When's the last time you saw Mary?"

"You mean now? Or before?" She continued chomping and answered both. "Before this, I saw Mary at the Wyoming Belles contest ... hmm, I don't know, two months back? We stayed together then with about half these girls. More recently, I saw her last night at dinner with everyone else. I'm not staying in her room, so I didn't see her after that."

"Do you know who might have?"

"Tarryn is her bunkmate."

"Isn't Tarryn expected to take second place?"

"Sure, if you're a betting woman and you want to play it safe." Lauren flashed her pink-painted smile at me. "But if you really want to bet, go for me. I know I can do this."

"I'm sure you can. Did Mary seem okay at dinner?"

"I don't know. She was one of those quiet types — the really nice kind, you know? Like, she was *actually* nice and not faking it. I don't really get it."

"What about Tarryn? Did she seem okay? Were the two friends?"

"Tarryn is ... I mean, the girl wants to win. We all do. Were they best friends? Probably not. Were they civil enough? Oh, sure. We all are. There're only a few enemies among us, but I don't think Mary had any."

I processed the information, wondering if any of the girls had it in her to kill one of their own for a shot at winning. "Was anyone acting strangely this week? Especially last night or this morning?"

"Of course," she said. At my confused look, she shrugged. "We all act strange. We've each got these superstitions before a contest and, well, for example, Billie Jo pulls her eyebrows out from stress! The poor thing has to pencil them in."

I realized Billie Jo's eyebrows had seemed dark and stiff in an odd way, but as I wasn't an eyebrow aficionado, I'd looked right past it. "Anything else? Anything suspicious?"

"Girl, I'm so self-absorbed I don't notice much about others." Lauren stood. "I'm getting fried to a crisp. Can you talk to someone else now?"

I had Lauren send the next girl out, a sweet little Texas belle so nervous she hiccuped through the interview. I put her out of her misery and ended our chat early. I went through seven more interviews in similar fashion, startled to find how self-absorbed some of these ladies became during contest season. For crying out loud, eighteen women were staying in one big house and none of them had noticed a thing out of the ordinary.

When interviewee number ten strode out onto the porch with her long legs working like stilts, her head tilted high, her black hair swinging halfway down her back, I sat up with interest.

Tarryn Southland, the expected runner-up to the pageant queen. I knew from the other girls that she was full of country charm. Hailing from a small town in Alabama, she was the opposite of Marilyn in many ways. While Mary was bright and bubbly with piano playing as a talent, Tarryn was darker and quiet, known for her soulful singing voice.

"I didn't do it, if that's what you're wondering." Tarryn wore dark skinny jeans despite the warmth and humidity. She folded her legs like a crane beneath her as she sat. "I know y'all must think I'm guilty or that I wanted her dead because she was expected to win it all."

"I am trying not to assume anything," I said. "I'm just asking questions and following where the facts and evidence lead."

She gave me a bland smile. "That's all good, I suppose."

"Can you tell me more about Marilyn?"

"We all called her Mary," she said in that accent of hers. It was endearing in a gentle, kitschy way. "She was truly a nice girl. Seriously nice. You know, the kind who doesn't have enemies."

"So I've heard."

"I bet that makes it hard to find out who might've wanted her dead." Tarryn gave a dry smile, though her eyes had dampened. "The girl didn't deserve that. None of us did, but especially not Mary."

"I'm sorry for your loss." I hesitated, looking at the natural beauty. She'd foregone most makeup, but it seemed the rest of the girls hadn't bothered to put their beauty routines on hold for something as small as a murder. Could she be trying harder than the others to appear sympathetic because she had something to hide?

She sniffed, reached into her pocket and pulled out a tissue. Making an effort to shield her face from me, she dabbed at her eyes and blew her nose before turning back and apologizing. "Sorry about that."

"It's fine, of course. It must be hard for you girls. I have to ask, Tarryn, where were you at eight o'clock this morning?"

"Sleeping." She shrugged. "Apparently Mary wasn't, though, which means I don't have an alibi. The two of us were roommates. Danielle and Stacey will be rooming with us when they arrive, but their ferry was late getting to the island, so they hadn't joined us yet."

I remembered Danielle and Stacey missing from Coconuts the previous evening. My mind leaped to the worst possible conclusion; it was strange how quickly my brain had devolved into a paranoid spiral now that I knew a murderer lurked in Eternal Springs. "Do you think they stayed away because they knew something bad was going to happen?"

Tarryn frowned. "No, I don't think so. I haven't even met the girls before. They're sisters, and they're coming together. Mary said she hadn't met them but was excited to welcome them. She always did that."

"Did what?"

"Welcomed the girls," Tarryn said. "That's why it's so weird she's the one who ended up dead. No matter how many pageants she won — fifty-nine if you're counting — she never let it go to her head. I just don't think any of the girls could've hated Mary enough to ... ."

"To kill her?"

She nodded. "That strange-looking woman with all the plastic surgery said she was strangled."

I smiled at her description of Abigail. "She was, sadly. It

makes me wonder if it was someone she knew. Otherwise how could the murderer have gotten so close without her screaming? One scream and the house would have been alerted."

"I just wish she'd had time to scream," Tarryn said. "I would've run out and helped her."

Finding myself nodding solemnly along, I looked down at the notebook in my lap now littered with scribbles. "Thanks for your time, Tarryn. Just one more question. Well, two, I suppose. Was Mary acting strange at all? Did she seem different or stressed?"

Tarryn thought for a long minute. When she spoke, she bit her lip and stared into space. "Not that I can think of. I mean, I can't say for certain, you know? She pretty much kept her personal life to herself. We were different. I'm from the south, she was from New Jersey."

"New Jersey?" I hadn't heard that from the other girls. "That's right across the way."

Tarryn nodded, shrugged. "Guess so."

"And you didn't hear her get up this morning?"

"I thought you only got two more questions." Tarryn stared me down, starting to look annoyed. I'd obviously begun to wear out my welcome. But she sighed and continued. "No, okay? I sleep with a mask on and earplugs. Beauty sleep, you ever heard of it?"

A part of me wondered if that was a dig, but I tried not to take it to heart. "Okay, I know I said two, but I have one more."

"You want to know if I have any ideas about who killed her?" she asked, and I nodded. "I have no clue. Like I said, you're barking up the wrong tree talking to the girls in the house. Carl would probably know more."

"Carl?"

She gave me a stare that said I hadn't done my research.

"Her coach. Carl Hadley? He's, like, the most famous beauty pageant coach in the world."

"Is he staying on the island?"

"Your questions just never end, do they?" she retorted. When I gave her a pleading look, she sighed. "Yeah, just down the street. Whatever the heck that hotel is named. Eternal something or other."

I knew it. I thanked Tarryn and let her rejoin the rest of the girls while the last few contestants came out to speak with me. Stacey and Danielle hadn't arrived, which meant I had only six more after Tarryn. I made it through the lineup quickly. There wasn't much more to learn from the girls except that most of them were a sobbing mess who were seriously concerned their mascara had smudged.

By the time I let Ciara from Oklahoma rejoin the contestants, I was exhausted. It'd been a long, arduous process to interview each of the women, and while I'd been holed up here I couldn't help but wonder how far Skye had gotten with her investigation.

Surely, she'd already heard about Carl, which meant if I wanted to get to him first I'd have to move quickly. I found Billie Jo, thanked her again for her help in wrangling the pageant contestants, and wished her luck.

"Actually," I paused with a frown. "Is the beauty contest still taking place?"

"It's a pageant, not a contest," Billie Jo corrected. "And of course it is. The show must go on. Mary would have wanted what's best for us, and that's what's best."

Still chewing on that, I left the cottage and headed toward Eternal Springs's largest hotel. As I walked, I couldn't keep my mind from lingering on the one thing Tarryn had said that didn't quite match with anything else: *I just wish she had time to scream.*

I suppose that Tarryn could've been guessing. It wasn't a

horrible guess, as a matter of fact, but it niggled at me in a way that had me wondering if there was something else to it. The way she'd said it almost sounded as if she'd known more than she let on. Even if she wasn't guilty, had she seen something? Why hadn't Mary screamed?

Six

Eternal Springs Spa and Report was a fashionable little place that assisted the spa and resort in luring tourists to the island. Luckily, I was friendly with Leslie Harris, the woman who worked the reception desk. She pointed me toward Cottage Number Eight as the lodging of Mary's former coach, with a whisper to keep things quiet.

I strolled through the well-manicured lawn with its tropical trees and lush gardens sprawling in every direction. The ocean glistened a crystal blue in the distance while pools of deep, gemstone green lined the walkways. I followed a cobblestone path to a rope bridge, climbed over a small moat that separated the main hotel from the individual cottages, and squinted to locate number eight.

Number eight turned out to be the cottage closest to the ocean, with the most gorgeous of views. Carl must be making some good money coaching his contestants to be able to reserve prime real estate during one of the peak tourist seasons.

I wove along the sandy path and hesitated just outside the

front door. It wasn't as if things were exactly secluded out here — we were in part of the hotel and resort — but I was reminded again of Tarryn's odd observation. *Mary hadn't even had time to scream.*

Quite possibly, this meant she'd known her attacker. She probably wouldn't have cried out if Carl approached her — realizing only too late that he hadn't been there to help her, but to end her. I swallowed over the lump in my throat as the first wave of true fear washed over my body. It'd been delayed in coming, the shock of finding Mary's body had been stunted in a daze of activity. Now that it'd hit, goosebumps freckled across my skin.

My day had been so hectic I hadn't had time to think about anything except the mysterious elements surrounding Mary's murder. The puzzle, the clues, the potential reward for Hex 66.6's ratings if I could somehow unravel this whole thing. But in doing so, I now realized, I'd have to speak with a murderer. And if the murderer suspected I was onto him or her ... .

"May I help you?" The door opened to reveal a slim, coiffed gentleman dressed in a sharp suit.

"Carl?" I extended my hand. "I'm so sorry for your loss. My name is Evian Brooks, and I'm helping with the investigation into Mary's death."

The gentleman cleared his throat, looking slightly bemused. "I'm sorry, ma'am. I am not Carl. He's resting now. I'm his personal assistant. May I deliver your message to him?"

"I really would prefer to speak with him myself. It's urgent."

The assistant cast an uncomfortable glance over his shoulder. "I really think he should rest, Miss Brooks. There was another woman here earlier asking questions and it upset him dreadfully."

"Aw, crap. Skye?"

"You know her?"

"Sort of," I said, cringing. I couldn't complain much because I technically had no authority to go around snooping into other peoples' business. I could call myself some sort of investigative reporter, but if the cops caught wind of my snooping they wouldn't be pleased. "We're both, ah, helping look into the murder."

"It's tragic, but maybe another time when he's —."

"John, who is it?" The voice croaked from another room, sounding quite ill. "Someone about Mary's murder? I don't want to talk to them."

"But sir, it's important," I said. "We're trying to find who killed her."

Silence. Then a long sigh. "Let her in, John."

"But sir," the assistant said, "you told me yourself you wanted to rest."

"Let her in. A few more questions won't kill me." The room fell quiet at his poor choice of words. Then sobs came from the bedroom, which made Carl's assistant look quite alarmed.

"Go on in," he said. "I'll bring you both some tea."

I wove through the small, bungalow-style cottage toward Carl's voice. The bedroom turned out to be a luxurious room, adorned in sea greens and pristine whites, decorated with shells and sand dollars and driftwood picture frames.

"I'm so sorry to barge in," I said, and I meant it. Stopping at the entrance, I knocked to be polite since the door was already open. "I'll try to keep this brief."

"I don't see how it won't be." Carl paused for a huge honk of his nose into a handkerchief. "There's not much I can add to what I told the other woman."

I inched forward, hands folded before my body. Carl truly looked as if he was in the firm grip of pain. He wore a white linen shirt and had the bedcovers pulled up to his waist. Judging by his assistant's style, I ventured a guess that Carl normally took pride in his appearance. He probably wouldn't let his hair go all mussed as it was now, nor would he be caught dead in his pajamas.

"I'm sorry for my appearance," Carl said, gesturing to himself. He must have caught me staring. "I would never allow anyone to see me like this, but ... alas, circumstances."

"Tell me a little about Mary, please," I said. "How did you meet, how long you've known her, things like that."

"We met when she was twenty-one." He gave a watery smile. "Ten years ago already, can you imagine?"

I placed Carl to be in his late thirties, possibly early forties, with preliminarily gray hair. Save for the pajamas and rumpled look, he resembled most businessmen we saw in Eternal Springs lounging away on holiday from their office jobs.

"I picked her out of a contest," he said with a little grin. "She finished seventh, but I knew she had it in her to be a winner. With a bit of coaching and ten years of practice ... *voila.*"

"Fifty-nine wins," I said, proud of my beauty pageant knowledge. "Quite impressive."

"Yes, though sixty ... ." He paused for a sob that wracked his shoulders. "Sixty would have been a huge cause for celebration. Now she'll never get to see the day."

"Did you see Mary quite often?" I asked. "Had her mood changed at all lately?"

"I saw her every day, sometimes twice a day. We rehearsed questions, practiced etiquette and of course spent hours tooling around on the piano to improve her talent."

"What about her mood?"

"You mean, did she vary from being the sweet, wonderful woman that everyone knew?" He shook his head. "No, never.

I don't know how anyone could dream of murdering her. I heard she was strangled. How ... how horrible! I can't imagine what that might have been like for her."

"I'm sorry to ask this, Mr.—," I hesitated.

"Just call me Carl."

"Carl," I said. "But where were you between seven and nine this morning?"

Carl sat up straighter in bed, turning his eyes to look straight at me for the first time. "Are you asking for my alibi?"

"It's standard procedure for anyone near the victim," I told him. "I'm sorry, but —."

"I was waiting for her down at Coconuts," he said. "You can verify with the bartender who let us in. She never showed."

"Coconuts?" I asked. "Isn't it a little early for drinks?"

He rolled his eyes. "They're setting up the pageant, so we couldn't rehearse in our normal space on stage. The bar has a keyboard for karaoke nights that they agreed to let us practice on before they opened."

I nodded, making a note to check his alibi. I doubted he'd lie over something so easily verified, but I'd rather be safe than sorry — and what's more, I could use a drink after the day I'd had.

"I'm sorry, ma'am." The assistant had returned. "I'm going to show you out, now. He's not feeling well and doesn't have anything more to add."

"Do you have any idea who might have wanted Mary dead?" I asked the coach. "Were any of the girls jealous?"

Carl's head sagged into his lap. "I don't know! I don't see how any of the other contestants could have the heart to strangle her, but I just don't know."

"Who made the decision for the show to go on?" I asked. "I thought it might be cancelled."

"Well, Edwin, of course," Carl said, blinking his eyes to

look at me. "The coordinator. If you haven't talked to him yet, you should. He's the one benefitting from all of this. There's no publicity like a murder to drum up interest, is there?"

Seven

After I took my leave from Carl, I opted to skirt the main road in favor of the more scenic route. The day had passed in a blur. I'd been so attuned to the murder that I'd forgotten to do basic things like eat and drink, so I figured a quick trip to Coconuts was in order.

My growling stomach told me it was almost dinner time, so when I slid onto my normal stool at the tiki bar I wasn't surprised to find the place was already filling with people. I put in my usual order for fish tacos, and then opted for a special occasion margarita because I was done working for the day.

As I waited for the food to arrive, I sat quietly, reflecting on everyone I'd spoken to in the last ten hours. I'd interviewed most of the contestants, the medical examiner and Mary's coach. I'd been grilled by Kenna, accosted by Mason and was half-starved from all my running around the island. I just might have a second margarita.

Then again, I still had things to do. I really should stop by the shop to offer my grudging thanks to Mason for taking care of my scooter. Maybe if I sucked up extra nicely I'd get some sort of buy one-get one free deal. I was no specialist, but it looked like my poor vehicle had been through hell.

When my food arrived, I ate it slowly, watching the bar fill rapidly with the dinner crowd. About half of the beauty pageant contestants were here, which gave the room a subdued feel. They picked at their food and tended to not eat, and they looked forlornly at one another with their perfectly made-up faces.

Publicly they mourned in such a way one would've thought they were all sisters. I wondered if any of the beautiful women hiding behind lipstick and coiffed hair and fake-tanned skin had murdered their fellow contestant. And for what? For a chance at winning a stupid beauty contest?

"Not how I thought the night would go," Mason said, sliding onto a bar stool next to me. "It's like the party died, wouldn't you say?"

I gave him a scowl as I turned his way. "Too soon, Mason. In poor taste."

"Sorry."

I continued scowling until I realized that I was supposed to be sucking up to the mechanic. Glancing at my plate, I debated offering him one of my tacos, but that ship had sailed. All of said tacos had made their way into my stomach, as had half the margarita.

"Can I buy you a drink?" I asked. "As a thank-you for your help?"

Mason looked ready to decline on habit, but he changed his mind. "Sure — Corona, please."

The bartender nodded that he'd heard and slid us the opened bottle. Mason caught it, raised his beer and clinked my margarita.

"What could we possibly have to cheer?" I asked as I took a sip of my drink. "What a disaster of a day."

"To dinner with friends."

I studied him for a moment, wondering where this burst of *friend* talk had come from. Mason and I had clashed several times in high school and had not made our way out of it unscathed. I barely remembered what we'd fought over back then, but the touchy balance had lingered.

"To dinner with friends," I said, clinked again, and took another sip. "What are you doing here?"

"I always come in for taco night." He popped his beer onto the counter with a grin. "I know you do too. You just never see me. It's okay, I'm easy to ignore."

My face colored. The truth was that he wasn't easy to ignore. It was as if my body had a weird signal that turned itself toward Mason whenever he was in the room, a little siren that alerted me to his presence whether I wanted to ignore him or not.

"I meant why'd you come and sit next to me?" I asked. "Do I look that desperate for a friend?"

"I hear you've been busy today. I thought you might want to talk about it."

"Who'd you hear that from?"

"Oh, you know ... ."

The answer stormed into the bar at that moment, her red hair snapping and crackling with frustration. "Are you trying to drive all the tourists away?" Kenna tapped her perfectly manicured nails against her clipboard as she stopped directly in front of me and hissed over my beer. "Asking questions, pestering — we don't even know for sure that this is a murder!"

"Yes, we do," I said evenly. "I talked to Abigail."

"She's part of the problem! All this talk about murder when maybe it was a horrible accident."

"Kenna, you know that's ridiculous. Mary was murdered. My asking questions about it has nothing to do with the number of tourists we attract."

"I'm on the tourism board! This is important, and I don't appreciate you making fun of it." Her eyes scanned the clipboard. "Seven people cancelled their ferry rides to Eternal Springs today. Seven people!"

"Seven less people to steal my tacos," Mason mumbled, looking around as if someone here had stolen his food. "It never takes this long to get a plate of tacos. If anything, we have too many people running around."

I was reminded of something Carl had said. "There's nothing like a murder to draw attention and a bigger crowd," I told Kenna. "If anything, we might get an influx of lookie-loos wanting to pop on over to our creepy little island and take a look around."

"It's not a creepy little island!" Kenna appeared horrified at the thought. "It's a lush, beautiful retreat. A place to relax and unwind, to unplug and treat yourself ... ." She stopped mid-sales pitch and sucked in a breath. "Oh, you're right. A little spin and the right article and I could change the way this thing goes. Have you seen Skye? I'll need her to print an article for me."

"Nope," I said. "She's probably off interviewing more people like I should be doing."

"Just do me a favor," Kenna said, breathless with new excitement. "Keep your investigation on the down low, will you? People are talking."

"I'll make you a deal," I said, watching as her eyes connected with mine with glittering interest. "I'll make a big effort to be more discreet if you help me out with Zola."

"What about Zola?" Kenna's eyes shifted to Mason, then back to me. We were all cautious not to reveal too much about our shared histories. "You know I rarely talk with her."

"But you're on good enough terms, yes?" I waited until she gave a reluctant nod. "If you can get her to help with my garden, I'll be so discreet people won't even know I'm looking into the case."

"What's wrong with your garden?" she asked. "Why do you need Zola?"

"She's got the whole green thumb thing going," I said pointedly. "My yard and plants are turning into this weird slushy thing and I can't figure out what's wrong. Paul won't even get his feet dirty."

"Yeah, well no offense, but Paul's a wuss," she said. "Sorry, but it's true."

I shrugged. "Fine, but still. Do we have a deal?"

She nodded.

"You know, Evian, it's not your duty to continue any sort of investigation." Mason reached over, rested a hand on mine and squeezed. "It's not your job to solve Mary's murder. It's not your fault you stumbled on the body."

"This isn't about Mary," Kenna snapped, then realized how horrible that sounded and backtracked. "I mean, it is — the poor woman — but if I could just find Skye, maybe we can turn this story around and salvage the beauty pageant."

Still muttering, she turned and floated out of the bar in her haze. We waited until she was gone before speaking. Mason was the first to break the silence.

"Interesting little woman, isn't she?" he asked with a raised brow. "What is it between the four of you, anyway? Zola, Kenna, Skye and you. I can't tell if y'all are friends or enemies."

"Join the club." I slumped closer to my margarita and took a sip. "It's complicated. We went to school together."

Mason frowned. "That convent, right? Didn't something happen there?"

"Yep."

"Not ready to talk about it?"

"Nope."

"Great. Let's talk about your day. Did you find anything out with all your interviews?"

"Oh, sure," I said, sounding forlorn and sarcastic. "Everyone loved Mary, and how could anyone want to kill her? Most people have some sort of strange alibi that doesn't quite clear them, though they're all believable enough. Oh, speaking of that, I have to ask the bartender a question."

I raised a hand, waited a few minutes until he slid my way and raised his eyebrows.

"Were you working this morning?" I asked. "Here, I mean?"

He nodded, then gestured toward my glass. "Yeah, need a refill on that?"

"Not yet." I pulled it closer, telling myself more margaritas wouldn't solve a murder mystery no matter how much I wanted it to be true. "This morning, do you remember if anyone was here when you opened?"

"Are you talking about that nut who asked to borrow the keyboard?" Jim raised his eyes. "Yeah, he was here for a bit. Why?"

"Just curious. Was he alone?"

"Yeah. Waiting for a girl to show, but she never did. Said he was some sort of coach." Jim shrugged. "He gave me a hundred bucks to sit here for an hour."

"What time was he here? And did he leave at all?"

"I just let him in — we didn't open until eleven, so I ran some errands and stocked up a new shipment. I didn't really see the dude at all."

I sighed. Another half-alibi. Carl hadn't lied about coming here, but the more I asked around the more it seemed impossible I'd ever find anyone who had a solid, rule-them-out alibi.

"Why you so interested? Is this to do with that murder that happened earlier?" Jim's eyes bugged out. "Are you asking me to provide an alibi for the guy? Jeez, Evian. I don't want that sort of pressure on me. Why are you poking around, anyway? Why not leave it to the cops?"

"She stumbled across Mary's body and feels guilty," Mason replied in a dry monotone. "Try to talk her out of getting involved. I already tried."

"Mary deserves justice," I said, "and I was the one to find her. It feels ... . I feel obligated to help her." That, plus the whole investigative piece for the station, but I didn't need to make that public. That made me sound as bad as Kenna.

"You could get hurt." Mason stared at me, more intense, more deeply than ever before. "Nobody wants to see you get hurt, Evian. Leave this to the professionals."

"You both are making such a big deal out of this. I'm only asking a few questions. I'm not planning to get hurt or in trouble, or any of that. Okay?"

Jim shrugged and disappeared down the bar to serve another customer. Mason didn't respond, sipping his beer instead.

"Why do you care, anyway?" I asked him. "Here I thought you got excited every time I found myself in a mess."

"Messes you can get yourself out of," Mason said, "but this time —."

"There you are." Skye interrupted. "I need to talk to you, Evian Brooks."

"Can't this wait?" While I wasn't excited to see Skye, I was particularly annoyed this time around because I wanted to hear what Mason had to say. "I'm in the middle of a conversation."

"You know what?" Mason said, standing. "You have a lot going on, Evian. I'll leave you to it. Your scooter — sorry, but it might take a week. You really pulled it through the wringer."

"Yes, yes," Skye waved him away. "Toodles. Hasta la vista."

"Bye," I called over Skye's shoulder as he walked away.

Turning to the wind witch, I glared. "Why are you ruining my dinner?"

Her eyes flicked to my empty plate. "Your food is gone. Nothing left to ruin. Jim, can I get a margarita?"

Jim nodded. We waited until he poured Skye's drink before she launched into her list of woes.

"I'm the investigative one in Eternal Springs," Skye said. "You're ruining the good thing I have going. Why are you interviewing all these people anyway?"

"I'm not ruining anything! You got to all of the people before I did."

"I know, but sometimes I have follow-up questions, and when I called to ask about them, they're all, like, 'I told your friend everything.'"

"Well, I haven't been telling anyone we're friends."

"Good. So, let me do my job, will you? You have the radio show. I have the newspaper."

"The radio has been stuck on calypso music ever since we … ." I lowered my voice, looking around the room. "Ever since that incident at school. You're part of the reason nobody listens to me!"

"Yes, well." Skye looked proud. "Just leave my witnesses alone."

"They're not your witnesses, and you are not a cop. I am conducting an investigative piece on it too — I just don't write about it. I am talking about it on air."

She rolled her eyes. "On a station nobody listens to."

"Maybe they will listen when I find out who murdered Mary before you!" A few nearby glances flicked our way, and I lowered my voice. "Also, I sincerely don't appreciate your little wind gimmick this morning with the storm."

Skye grinned. "I thought it was quite clever."

"You sent gale force winds my way, made me late for work and sent me spiraling almost face first into the same pool as a dead body," I said. "That's hardly a prank. It's overkill."

"Overkill." She snickered. "Good one."

"Can you never let one of my projections be correct? I just wanted one sunny day without wind or rain."

"Okay, I had nothing to do with the rain ... really," she shrugged. "I just blew in a few breezes, so yeah, maybe that was my fault. But the bit about you wiping out on your scooter and crashing through the fence was not my fault. I can't help it if you don't know how to steer straight."

"Lay off the weather patterns or I'll drench the little notebook you carry around writing all your stories in!"

She frowned but seemed to agree to a truce for the time being. "If you want my advice —."

"I don't."

"Lay off the interviews. Leave it to the professionals."

"Like the police?"

She didn't seem to have an answer to that one, so in response she slurped down the rest of her margarita, turned and stormed out. I stood with a huge sigh, realizing both Mason and Skye had flounced in, had dinner and left me to foot the bill. And I already had a huge bill with Mason. Just wait until I got my hands on him!

"Nah, you're all good," Jim said when I threw enough money on the table to cover all our food and drinks. "Mason took care of it."

"But —."

Jim nodded for me to pick up the cash. "It's all good."

"Did he tip you?"

"I told you he took care of everything," Jim said. "Have a good night, Ev. And maybe give the poor guy a break next time you see him. I think he likes you."

It was with that thought that I floated home, blissfully free from the rest of my worries such as murder, unpaid bills and malfunctioning scooters. As I twirled through my front door I saw Paul sitting on the kitchen table, watching me through narrowed eyes.

What are you so happy about? he asked. *I don't like it. Something is weird about you.*

"I'm not allowed to be happy?"

Not when you found a dead body this morning.

"Gee, you really know how to keep a party going."

What was it? Did you go to Coconuts without me? I smell salt and lime on you. Don't tell me you had a margarita and didn't bring me one.

"Paul, can't you just go outside and sit under a fern like a normal toad?" I studied my familiar fondly. Though we bantered, I couldn't imagine life without him. "You're the only toad in the world who takes cooling baths in margaritas."

His body gave a shudder of excitement at the thought. *Well, I'm not just any toad now, am I?*

I headed to the blender and gathered the ingredients for Paul's favorite: a strawberry margarita with a sugared rim. Next he'd be asking for a bon bon. It was all very *If You Give a Mouse a Cookie* with this one.

So, he said as I rubbed the lime around the rim of the glass, *what's got you all peppy?*

I debated a massive attempt to keep my thoughts hidden from Paul, but that would never fully work. The moment my guard dropped he'd be able to read my thoughts anyway.

"I think Mason doesn't hate me," I told Paul. "And he might give me a deal on the scooter."

I don't know about the deal on the scooter, but of course the man likes you. He's been drooling after you since you ran into his garage on that golf cart.

"Let's not talk about that," I said, picking up Paul and plopping him into the margarita. "Maybe Skye did have a point — it's probably not her fault I crashed. But it is her fault the wind crapped my scooter out."

Paul gave a heavenly sigh, closed his eyes, and sat back to relax.

Go away. I'm basking.

I left my toad to bask and climbed upstairs to prepare for bed. After a quick shower and a few hours spent compiling and pouring over my notes from the day, I decided to turn in early.

Tomorrow morning I'd pay a visit to Edwin. Somebody had to know something about the murder. The only thing I could be certain of about this case was that poor Marilyn hadn't killed herself.

Eight

"Good morning," I chirped to Leslie, the receptionist at Eternal Springs Resort and Spa. Luckily Dylan, an overly hopeful kid with crushes on me and my witchy sisters, wasn't working today. I didn't have time for his bribes *or* his misplaced affection. "Brought you a coffee."

I handed over a to-go cup from the local coffee shop, earning a smile from her.

"And what do you need today?" she asked. "I can't send you back to Carl's room. His assistant put in a request for no more visitors. Apparently, the poor man's been bombarded by people after his friend died yesterday."

Lucky thing I'd made the cutoff, I thought, as I raised my own latte to my lips and took a sip. "Oh, no. It's just, actually, I have an interview request for the radio show. Do you know Edwin Prong's room number?"

Leslie leaned closer. "I'm really not supposed to be giving these things out to you."

I gave a pointed look at her coffee. "Well, in that case ... ."

Leslie hugged the coffee protectively with both hands.

"Fine, but I'm just going to point the room number out to you. If he doesn't want to talk, leave him alone. And make up some story about how you found his room, okay? I can't get fired. I need this job."

"Thanks so much," I said. "Oh, I really love you."

"You're just lucky I am addicted to coffee," she said, her eyes scanning her log. "Okay, here we are. You're headed to this room," she pointed to Room 809 on the screen. "Upstairs — not quite the penthouse, but a pretty sweet suite." She giggled at her own joke. "Sorry, hotel humor."

I laughed along with Leslie, an acquaintance old enough to be considered a friend. We didn't hang out all that often because keeping close human relationships is a bit of an issue for me. Sooner or later, they began to question why I talked so much to a toad or why I took so long to shower.

To answer the latter, it was due to the Coven. They tended to contact me — a hugely annoying process — through the bathroom mirror when it steamed up. Not exactly a relaxing steamy shower when a voice barked through the curtain for me to hurry up because I was late to a meeting.

I considered this as I walked along the corridor and took the elevator up to the eighth floor. I really needed to put a curtain over my mirror. I'd do that as soon as I got home — it'd been on my to-do list for three years.

The elevator dinged and I stepped onto an open-air corridor. Though I'd spent most of my life in Eternal Springs, I paused to take in the sights, to inhale a breath of the fresh air, to sip my coffee in an attempt to enjoy the morning. The views from eight floors up were unparalleled: In most directions, the ocean stretched for miles, disappearing as if fading into a watercolor landscape.

Tree branches obscured some of the view, but the grass

and underbrush washed the island with greenery. A golf course sat in the distance for the older men who got dragged along while their wives sat through every spa treatment under the sun.

Room 809 was a corner unit. I spotted the number as I finished the dregs of the magic potion known to humans as coffee. With a sigh, I dropped the cup into the nearest trash container and forced myself to raise a hand and knock before the caffeine rush wore off.

I'd done some asking around about Edwin as I'd grabbed the coffee this morning. A few of the pageant girls had been at the cafe, whispering over their black coffees and avoiding the pastries as if even a whiff of them would add inches to their thighs.

Most of the girls had run into Edwin at one point. His bio stated he was from New York, but upon closer inspection he had been born and raised in Iowa, though he tended to hide that branch of his roots. He now worked as a professional pageant coordinator and traveled often and widely, organizing staging, costumes and even distribution for televised programs.

One thing all the girls had agreed on was a lack of fondness for the man, which sent my gut churning as the door was pulled open by a harried-looking man with frustration in his eyes. I glanced up and down the hallway and realized, once again, that I was quite alone up here despite being in a public place. Not unlike Marilyn the morning she'd been killed.

"Yes?" he asked, sounding annoyed at the silence. "Are you housekeeping? Where's your uniform? I'm going to call the front desk to verify. I told them I am very private about my space."

"No — no," I said quickly. "It's not like that at all. My name is Evian Brooks, and I am an investigative reporter for HEX 66.6," I said, fudging just a little. Maybe the title wasn't professional yet, but if I did a good enough job on this case I could promote myself. "I just have a few questions."

Edwin's eyes flashed darker. "Your name is Evian, like the bottled water?"

"The one and only." I tried to stay positive. "Unfortunately, I'm here about Marilyn."

"Marilyn." He thought for a little too long on the name before it registered. "Oh, Mary. Yes — poor girl. But I already talked to a woman about her last night."

I muttered a silent curse to Skye, reminding myself to set a spell on her shower that would make the water come out glittery. She'd hate that. "She's with the newspaper, I'm with the radio. Please, just a moment of your time."

"I don't know what else I can add, but come in, I suppose. You're not going to talk about any of this on air, are you?"

"Not if you prefer I don't. Eventually I'd like to report on the murder when we find the killer, but I can keep anyone who wouldn't like their name shared anonymous."

He gestured for me to get started. While I asked him my first few questions about how long he'd known Mary, where they'd met, he fluttered around the kitchenette and popped a K-cup into the coffee machine.

"I met her — it must be five years ago at least? Sometime after Carl plucked her from obscurity and helped her to start winning. See, I don't work with the girls that much except when it comes to staging. In fact, I barely know any of their names unless they're a winner."

"But you did know Mary?"

"I mean, I knew of her. Met her a few times, yes. The girl's won, like. Sixty —."

"— Fifty-nine," I corrected, then explained when he looked confused. "Fifty-nine. It's sort of a big thing she didn't make it to sixty wins."

"Whatever. She won all the time, so yes, we'd talked. Would I call us friends? No. Friendly acquaintances? Sure."

"When's the last time you saw —," I paused as Edwin smacked the top of the K-cup machine. The pounding lasted for a solid minute until the thing kicked into gear and began sputtering water. "When was the last time you saw Mary?"

He squinted. "I don't know, I guess a month ago at the Nashville show? I think I read she'd won something in Wyoming or Utah after that, but I didn't coordinate it so I didn't pay much attention."

He spoke with a haughtiness that made me think he was convinced nobody else could measure up to him. His shows were the best, and he clearly didn't much care for any competition.

I wondered if I should be checking out some of his competition — if the show in Utah or Wyoming had been a huge, raging success, might he have killed Mary to get more eyeballs on this one? It would certainly bring a level of notoriety. With notoriety comes attention and eyeballs, and once again, Edwin would be the center of it all.

"Did you ever have any issues with Mary?" I asked. "Any clashes?"

"Do you think I killed her?" He smacked the K-cup machine one more time and stared angrily into his cup. "What is this stupid thing, sludge?"

I winced. "Electronics here aren't really the best. But there's an excellent coffee shop —."

"I don't have time to go buy coffee," he snapped. "I have a beauty pageant to run. I have things to do, places to be, people to organize. You think my job is easy?"

"No, of course not, I just meant ... ." I hesitated. "Sorry. Just a few more questions and I'll be out of your hair. Did you ever clash with Mary?"

"I didn't kill her!"

"That doesn't answer my question."

"I know who did clash with Mary. How about that?"

I squinted at him, trying to determine if he was trying to be helpful in his odd, stuck-up way, or if he was trying to divert my attention. Possibly both. "Who?"

"I think the video is still online," Edwin said, pulling out his phone and punching a few buttons. "Stupid internet here. Why is it so horrible? I can never get any service."

I wrinkled my nose, tempted to jokingly tell him it was all the magic whizzing around the place, but I didn't think he was in the mood for a joke. And he definitely wasn't interested in the truth.

"Here. You'll recognize her." Edwin held out his phone. "Video is low quality and the playback speed is horrendous, but it's all you need."

I squinted at the screen and studied the blurry video. The headline read: *Catty for the Crown!* As the clip rolled, I watched two women appear backstage, one of them — it looked like Mary, but a much younger version — strutted forward holding a bejeweled crown in her hand.

The second woman followed slightly behind and, when Mary wasn't looking, took a running leap that ended with a vicious piggy back. The second woman yanked at Mary's hair, and in response, Mary cried out and flailed. Before I could blink, the two contestants were wrestling over the crown.

"Who's the crazy one trying to steal the crown?" I asked. The static was terrible, and the pixels were the size of Saturn. "I can't see her face clearly."

"Wait ... ."

I waited for another few seconds, watching as the girls twisted and snarled on the ground. Mary didn't let go of the crown. The second woman sent a claw-like swipe at Mary's face, this time drawing blood as it scratched her cheek.

That's when I saw it: her face. I recognized that woman.

"Oh, my gosh!" I dropped the phone into Edwin's hand. "It can't be!"

He gave a cheeky little smile. "Still think I killed Mary?"

"I don't know what to think." I tried to hide my stunned reaction, but I couldn't quite manage. Backing away from the phone, I shook my head and tried to make sense of what I'd seen.

"That was before all her plastic surgery," Edwin said, flipping the phone around to face him. "She was a real looker back then, as you can see. In fact, she could've really been something. It could have been her out there winning sixty —."

"Fifty-nine."

"— pageants instead of Mary."

"But that means … ." I hesitated and looked up at Edwin. "That would mean our very own medical examiner had a motive to murder Mary."

He nodded and gave a grim, although not entirely un-gleeful, smile. "That was my first thought when I heard the news. Of course, I knew Abigail had come to live in Eternal Springs as a form of exile from the rest of the world. She was so embarrassed after this video went viral that she gave up her pageant career entirely and became a plastic surgeon. That had always been her backup plan."

I blinked, oddly intrigued to find that Abigail and I were both stuck here in our own way. Her, in exile from embarrassment, me, to save the world. Still, we were both here because of unfortunate pasts.

"She was the first one at the crime scene." I looked up at Edwin, aware I should keep my mouth shut, but unable to do so. "She was there, and she had this smile on her face."

"Let me guess, no alibi?" Edwin shrugged. "Jealousy and revenge are strong motivators. Especially when she's the one in charge of the evidence and the autopsy."

"I've got to find her," I said. "Sorry to barge in here, but ... oh, can I ask you one more thing?"

"Where was I yesterday morning?" Edwin gave a complicated smile. "Right here, trying to work this stupid coffee machine."

Nine

I set out to find Abigail, reluctant to head straight back to the spa where she'd likely be getting one treatment or another to kick the day off. I had promised Kenna that I'd stay low key for the time being — assuming she was working on getting Zola's cooperation for our deal.

On the way out I stopped by the reception desk again. Leslie was taking a last sip of the latte I'd brought her. Coming around to face me, she dropped the to-go mug in the trash and smiled. "How'd everything go?"

"Great!" I said too cheerfully. "Say, I have an unrelated question to ask you. As a friend, this time."

"Your last favor was as a friend." She pursed her lips, hovering on the edge of dismay. "I told you, Evian. I can't keep doing this for you. That was the last favor. People are going to start asking questions."

"See, this isn't actually about getting into someone's room. It relates to the spa." I rested my hands on the desk and gave a shifty look in both directions. "You have clients who come here wanting procedures done, but also wanting to keep things private, right?"

"All the time! Probably about eighty percent of our clients. Though, of course, one-hundred percent are kept confidential. We don't leak the secrets of beauty to the universe."

A nifty little tagline that probably made all those booking their procedures feel extra warm and fuzzy with the added security measures. "That sounds perfect," I drawled. "And didn't I read somewhere that free consults are offered for those of *us* who might want something done?"

"Oh, are you finally going to get that nose fixed?!" Leslie reached out and gave me a cute little *boop* on a nose I thought was perfectly fine. "We can smooth that bump right out."

I ran a hand protectively over my apparently-bumpy nose. "Ah, no. My nose is fine. Er, I thought it was anyway, but sure, what the heck? Any chance Abigail has an opening today? I'd prefer the best."

"Abigail is the best," Leslie trilled happily. "Let me see when she can fit you in. Look at that! How does twenty minutes from now work? We had a cancellation."

"Perfect." I exchanged information with Leslie and received the location of the office. "Thanks a million."

With ten minutes to spare, I decided to pop out for another coffee. I grabbed a large burnt butterscotch latte with an extra shot of espresso. Something told me I'd need the jolt of energy the second Abigail stepped into the room and found me there instead of an actual paying client.

Indeed, she wasn't pleased when she arrived.

"What are you doing in my office?!" Abigail stepped into the small, modern room, tapping her clipboard against her leg. "I thought I asked you to stay away from me. And if I didn't, I should have. You gave me the Spanish Inquisition yesterday, and I'm done answering your stupid questions."

"It's just one more —."

Abigail ignored me, looking down at the clipboard a

second receptionist had handed her. "Oh, I'm sorry. Are you here for a consult on that bump?"

I blanched and rubbed my nose self-consciously. "What the heck is so wrong with my nose?"

"Well, it's just a bit *bulky*. And slightly misshapen."

"I use it to breathe!" I glanced in the mirror behind Abigail. "I don't really think it's so bad."

"Well, you're finally here for a consult, aren't you? You've seen the light, honey, and admitted you have a problem. That's the first step."

I wrinkled my problem nose at Abigail, surprised in the change of her candor when she thought I'd converted to plastic surgery. It might have been a testament to my acting skills — it couldn't actually be my nose was so horrible, could it? — that she believed me so quickly. "No, Abigail, I'm here to ask you some questions."

"Let me answer them for you." She seemed supremely happy about my need to ask questions, which was confusing until she began to answer them. "You will experience some bruising, some swelling. If you want to keep this under wraps — no pun intended — I might recommend scheduling a week or so off work. There will be some sensitivity, but I have no doubt you'll be pleased with the results."

"I'm here about the murder, Abigail."

"Don't be such a drama queen," she continued. "You won't die on my table." She stopped when understanding finally struck. "Oh, bollycocks! You aren't looking into changing that awful nose of yours at all, are you?"

Her disposition flipped in an instant. Her sunny smile deflated and her eyes flashed with frustration. "How dare you take up my time? Some helpless person could have really used this slot, Evian."

"A helpless person? Paying an ungodly sum of money for a

procedure that only changes the way they look? Pick a new word, Abigail. I wouldn't call them helpless."

"Feeling beautiful on the outside can completely change one's inner self," she said, her nose tilted upward. "Maybe you wouldn't know that because you're so plain, but I'm sure you can imagine what it might feel like to have a straighter nose."

I imagined, but it didn't get very far. I didn't care enough about the curvature of my breathing apparatus to pay an abominable sum to have it altered. "How dare I take up your time? How dare you lie to me?"

"I didn't lie to you."

"I'd call it a mighty big omission," I said. "You never disclosed you had a relationship with the victim."

"I didn't have a relationship —."

"I saw the video."

She frowned, put a finger to her inflated lips in thought. "Are you sure you wouldn't prefer to talk about your nose? I can give you quite a discount."

"Why did you hide that?"

"You're not the police, Evian." She stood and grimaced. "I am not required to talk to you."

"No, but I am going to go to the police and telling them all I've found." I hadn't sincerely planned to do any such thing because I figured between their own investigation and Skye's poking and prodding, the police were already ahead of me in their search for the murderer. "I suppose it doesn't make a difference, but at least I'm giving you the chance to explain yourself before I go."

She pulled back the hand that'd been reaching for the door. "Fine. What do you want to know? I'd met the victim. What about it?"

"You had a screaming match with her and a catfight that went viral on the internet. Then, you had to be convinced she'd been murdered in the first place because you're the only ME Eternal Springs has — and nobody's going to challenge you. Tell me something; if I hadn't been there and pointed out the strangulation marks, would you have even declared it a homicide?"

"Of course I would have." That odd little smile was back, and I couldn't help but wonder if in some way Abigail wasn't all that sad about Mary's death. Whether or not she killed her, Abigail didn't exactly seem concerned about the loss. "I just hate to make preliminary assumptions before I have all the information."

"Right." Though I didn't believe her for a second, I tried a new angle. "What was the fight about? In the video it looks like you tried to steal her crown."

"I know what it looks like, but really, the crown was rightfully mine. I was just trying to take it back."

"How do you figure that? Didn't she win?"

"Yes, but she cheated."

"How does one cheat in a beauty contest?"

"It's a pageant," she corrected, shuddering at my misuse of the phrase. "A pageant — not a contest. "She took diet pills."

"Don't most beauty contest — er, the ladies watch their diets?"

"Yes, but some pills are illegal in the pageant world. She was taking this medicine that offered huge results. Maybe if I'd been allowed to take them and have a size twenty-three waist I would've won."

"I thought the contests — pageants, sorry — weren't just about looks. There's the talent, and, er — whatever else you're judged on."

"Yes, yes, but Mary was very pretty and very talented. So was I, you know. It was a long time ago. And every inch from our hips mattered, I just know it. You weren't there, so you can't understand."

"No, I really can't," I said, having horrible visions of

parading myself around in a bikini and dancing with a flute to my lips. "That sounds horrendous."

"You know, you might have a chance if you actually spent some time grooming yourself. A little fix of your nose and — is that a butterscotch latte I smell? — yeah, you'd have to let those calories go. But ugh." She studied me. "You're naturally not so bad looking, but it doesn't mean you understand what it's like to be a beauty queen."

"I don't want to understand. I only want to know why you stole the crown from Mary."

"I told you. I found diet pills in her room, and they are *so* frowned upon. It's totally, like, copying homework or something in the back of the classroom from the smartest geek while everyone else slaves away figuring out their derivati-what-nots."

"Yesterday," I said, looking down at the tiny notebook I'd slipped from my pocket, "you never did say how you arrived at the crime scene so quickly."

Her back shot rigid. "What's it matter to you? I'm the ME on this stupid island. It's my job."

"That doesn't answer my question."

"How did you even find that stupid video?! Ugh!" She fanned her face as her cheeks turned pink with frustration. "Technology never works out here."

"Edwin's phone must have had a little cell reception juice left in it from the mainland," I said. "Or the video was cached or ... whatever! It doesn't matter. What matters is that you continuously dodge my question."

"I was there because I was in the neighborhood. There was a dead body and I popped on over."

"Nobody screamed," I said, parroting Tarryn's phrase. "How did you know?"

"I told you I was around!"

"Here's what I think happened. You were just *around*." I

shrugged, giving off an air of nonchalance that I wasn't truly feeling. "You swung by the house, maybe to greet the girls, maybe to scope out the scene. After all, you know what beauty pageants are like."

Her expression was stony as she watched me stand.

"Maybe you went inside and said hello to some of the girls." I paced back and forth, gave another bob of my shoulders. "All was well until you saw her. *Mary.*"

"I didn't —."

"I think that upset you because she took advantage of the system all those years ago with diet pills and stole the crown from you." I spun on a heel, turned to face Abigail and held out my hands as the murderer might have, fingers spread, headed for the throat. "You didn't mean to, but you were just so angry! Maybe you asked her to come outside with you to catch up, or maybe she was already out there and you surprised her while she was drinking her coffee."

"That's not —."

"Either way," I continued, gathering speed. "You found her, saw your opportunity and seized it. After all, the only person who'd examine the body is you. Even if there was evidence left behind, all it would take is a little … ." I made a flicking gesture. "Dump it in the trash and nobody is the wiser. At best, it's considered an accident, at worst, an unsolved murder by someone in a jealous fit of rage."

"Evian, stop! You —."

"Is that how it went?" Abigail shrunk under my raised voice, that smug smile finally wiped off her face. "Did you kill her because those sixty trophies should have belonged to you?"

"Evian!" Abigail screeched this time, bringing my accusations to a halt. "I was there for the freaking beauty samples!"

I did a double blink in surprise and stepped backward. "Excuse me?"

"The beauty samples!" She wiped a hand across her forehead, looking exhausted as she admitted it. "Evian, you're a stubborn little bulldog, you know that? I really am annoyed with you."

"What do you mean you were there for the beauty samples?"

"I mean that at these pageants — obviously you wouldn't know because you don't understand the first thing about beauty — ."

"We've established that," I cut in. "What about them?"

She shook her head and refocused. "Well, vendors come a week to a few days before the contest. They positively slather the girls in free stuff. Lotions, hair sprays, nail goodies, the latest and greatest in sleeping masks. You get the picture. They hand out curling irons and blow driers like aspirin. It's the place to be when trying to get hold of the best supplies in the industry."

"Huh," I said. "What do the companies get in return? Some sort of endorsement?"

"Of course you wouldn't understand this either because the island is stupidly horrible with technology — which is sort of good for me because the video remains somewhat hidden — but to everyone else in the country, or the world, social media is huge." She explained this to me as a teacher might detail two-plus-two for some foundering student. "Winners of beauty pageants become Instagram-famous. They get all these deals to promote products. Thousands, sometimes millions of impressionable young girls are seeing these posts."

"And all the vendors want their brands featured," I said. "So they show up, unload all their products, and then when the girls win they ask them to give their product a quick shout-out on social media."

"I mean, basically." Abigail rolled her eyes as if I hadn't

quite grasped the concept. "I knew the vendors might be there because the pageant is just days away. They need to start getting these products unloaded on the girls, stat! The ladies will start posting photos, their fans will ask what they used to get 'those fabulous curls,' and the vendors want the answer to be the name of their product."

"Did you find any of the vendors there?"

"Sure, a handful," she said with a wrinkled nose. "They were just setting up shop, though. You know pageant contestants, they need beauty sleep. One or two vendors had set up in the dining room."

"Did you go in there?"

"Well, yeah. I scored a new hair crimper and an eyeshadow palette. I wanted the face cream dude to fork over his supplies, but I think he suspected I wasn't actually a contestant. Stupid wrinkles."

I watched her dab at nonexistent crow's feet at the corners of her eyes and sighed. If Abigail thought she had wrinkles with all the Botox she did, my skin must look like an old leather speedbag. "What about the girls? I don't think any of them mentioned the vendors being around."

"Like I said, they were probably sleeping or primping or whatever. I arrived around eight fifteen. The vendors beat me there by a little bit."

"So they were there before the murder?" I asked, anxious. Maybe one of them had heard something or spoken to Mary. With a shudder, I wondered if one of them had been responsible for her death. "What time did they set up shop?"

"Gosh, I don't know specifics," she said, studying me carefully. "But I can't see why they would possibly have killed her. To answer your other question, I doubt any of the girls even knew vendors were around. They must have left sometime in the commotion of the murder because I was directing traffic away from the house."

"Why would you send people away?" I asked, furious. "You should have taken their statements!"

"I did. They didn't see anything," Abigail said, tapping her skull. "I remember every word up here."

"That's not your job; that's the police's job. Do you know how guilty this makes you look?"

"I'm telling you, I didn't kill her." Abigail leaned forward, her eyes narrowed. "In fact, I think love might be blinding you, missy. The answer might be closer than you think."

"What?"

"That little boy toy of yours is hiding something from you."

"Boy toy?" My dating life was a big fat goose egg at the moment, so I struggled to think of who she meant. My first thought was Paul, but I didn't think Abigail was quick enough to use Paul as an insult. "What are you talking about?"

"I saw you canoodling with Mason at Coconuts yesterday," she said with a snide grin. "Yeah. And he seemed pretty comfortable talking to you at the crime scene. Not to mention, he just 'took care' of that scooter for you? Yeah, right. You're not fooling anyone — Mason's not that nice."

"We're just friends," I said, hesitant. "If that. We've never been anything more."

"No, but I have." Abigail flipped a hand through her hair and tossed the locks over her shoulder. "We dated for quite some time. It was pretty serious, I'll have you know."

I sighed. Another checkmark in the "con" column for a guy I'd just begun thinking of as friendly. "That's too bad."

"It is, isn't it? I broke up with him," she said quickly, though the way her eyes darted away I wasn't sure if that was the truth. "That's how I can tell he's after you. He likes you, Evian, but you'd better watch what you get yourself into. He might be a murderer."

"How do you figure that?" I asked. "I was talking to him

right before my bike slipped and crashed into the crime scene."

"Yeah, I know. You've said as much." Abigail gave a proud sniff. "But what you haven't considered is why Mason was out and about anyway? If I remember, it was raining hard, he was just walking around? I'm sorry, nobody just goes for a stroll in a near hurricane. And he wasn't wearing jogging clothes. I know because I checked him out. He had on those jeans that make his butt look fabulous."

I held up a hand like a shield. "Don't need to hear that level of detail."

"See what I mean? You're letting love blind you." Abigail rested her hand on the doorknob and twisted. "If you weren't, maybe you'd have figured out his connection to Mary."

"What was his connection?" I asked, curious for an ex-girlfriend's point of view on the relationship.

"They dated for some time." Abigail watched my expression melt into one of surprise. "Yep, exactly. Then he was seen wandering around the murder scene of one of his many — so very many, I'll have you know — ex-girlfriends."

I swallowed and came up empty for a retort.

"Why do you think he's buttering you up?" She gave a tinkling laugh. "You didn't actually think he liked you, did you?"

"Um—"

"You saw him at the crime scene." She pulled open the door and stepped through, turning back to face me. "Now, you're asking questions, investigating and whatnot. Don't you see his plan? He's distracting you. Poor, quiet little Evian, who hasn't had a date in years. See how far a bit of flattery got that schmuck? You didn't even see what was right before your eyes."

Abigail turned away and clicked off, her heels sounding like angry tick-tocks against the floorboards as she walked.

My fingers clenched and unclenched in frustration, and my mind swam with knowledge, accusations, lies and half-truths.

I stormed out of the examination room and down the hallway. It irked me that Abigail had gotten the best of me once again. I'd been so sure there'd been more to the story with her than dumb old beauty samples, but again, she'd turned the tables. I was just as lost as before.

To make matters worse, it grated on me that Abigail might have a point. Had I been blind? Was it true I'd turned away from all the obvious signs of Mason's involvement in the case because he'd shown the slightest bit of interest in me?

I tried to convince myself that wasn't true, but I remembered the warmth I'd felt when he'd paid the bill yesterday. The huge wave of relief that I'd construed as kindness when he'd offered to take care of my scooter at the crime scene so I could get to work. Because he'd "buttered me up," as Abigail said, I hadn't even asked why he'd been out walking on a rainy morning just blocks from a crime scene.

With new determination, I headed for Mason's mechanic shop. I might've been too relaxed the first time through my questioning, but this time I'd make up for it.

All of these partial lies and missing pieces of information had me more convinced than ever that the true murderer was in our midst. Possibly, someone I knew. Possibly, a friend of mine. If I didn't find the killer soon, the chances were good he or she might kill again.

Ten

"What were you doing walking around in the rain?" I stormed straight into Mason's shop without pausing for niceties. "Why'd you pay the bill at dinner last night?"

Mason looked up from a golf cart he'd been tinkering with and gave me a crooked smile. "How many of those have you had today?"

He nodded toward the latte in my hand, and I realized I was trembling a little. Whether it was a caffeine overdose or a case of the angry jitters, I couldn't tell for sure. It was probably both.

"None of your business," I said, but I set the latte on the counter so he couldn't see my trembling fingers. "Answer me, Mason."

He took his time standing upright, facing me with a moderately amused look on his face. As he wiping hands stained with grease against his light-blue, well-worn jeans, I couldn't help but notice the way his arm muscles tightened under the black T-shirt, or the way his tanned skin practically glowed from all the time he spent in the sun.

With a pained bitterness, I realized that Abigail might be right. Here I was having these nice, friendly feelings that bordered on the romantic toward Mason, and he was using it to distract me from his involvement in a murder. Allegedly.

I had to prove him guilty as much as I would anyone else, but that didn't feel fair — I wanted to be angry with him. It had been so long since I'd given any man a chance that this felt like a bigger letdown than it should — and I wasn't even sure the feelings were reciprocated.

"Take a breath," he said, extending his hands toward me. He stepped across the floor of his garage and moved toward where I stood in front of the counter. "And back up. What are you getting at?"

I did as he said and breathed, though it felt exceptionally shallow. The air smelled of grease and motor parts, though not unpleasantly so. As Mason inched closer, I caught a hint of fresh, outdoorsy cologne. "I came here to ask you a few questions."

"All right, then. Go ahead. No need to have a heart attack while you're at it."

I barely refrained from making a face, but that was probably the caffeine. Not that I needed it, but I picked up the latte and took another swig for courage. "Yesterday morning, you were out walking around. Why?"

"Fresh air?"

"It was raining! You were wearing jeans. People don't wear jeans to get exercise — that's, like, the worst idea ever. I don't even need to exercise to know that for a fact."

He laughed. "I like a nice morning stroll after my first cup of coffee."

"Fine. But you're evading that question. What about the crime scene? You appeared there quite quickly."

"Right. Because I watched you skid halfway down the hill and crash through bushes and a fence." His look was almost patronizing. "I half expected you to be dead when I got there. I was doing the decent human thing to check on you and see if you needed help."

"Oh, yes, a real knight in shining armor."

The look of amusement was rapidly fading from his face. "Look, Evian, I'm humoring you answering these questions, but you haven't given me any reason to talk to you about Mary. You're not the police, nor the ME, nor a detective."

"Right, and you've dated at least two of the three parties you just mentioned."

"Is that what this is about?" He raised a hand, ran it across his eyes in a tired motion. "You found out about my relationship with Mary and now you think I killed her?"

"Not only her, but Abigail."

"What are you talking about? I never had a relationship with Abigail."

"Sure you did. Don't bother lying. She told me about it," I said. "And about the one with Mary. Had Mary moved on? Were you upset about it? Is that why you killed her?"

"I didn't kill anyone." Mason's voice was deadly calm. There was a fury burning just behind his eyes, but he didn't let it seep through — not yet. "I'd never hurt a soul. I fix things. I put them back together."

"You still haven't said why you were out wandering the streets on a rainy morning when a murder was committed just a block away."

"Fine. You want the story? I'll give it to you. But I don't think you'll like it." Mason crossed his muscled arms across his chest and leaned against the wall. If he weren't so terrifying at the moment, he'd be drop-dead gorgeous. "I never had what you'd call a 'relationship' with Abigail. She sat at my table one night at Coconuts and tried to feel me up. When she dove in for a kiss, I turned my head and she hit my cheek. Her ego was bruised after that, so she left me alone, but has been telling everyone that we had a serious relationship and she broke it off. Of course, I'm heartbroken and lost and lonely without her."

Mason looked none of those three things and, frankly, I could see Abigail pulling all aspects of the stunt. I shivered as he continued.

"The bit about Mary — yes, we had a relationship," he said. "It wasn't serious. That was the problem. We went out for six months or so, but during that time we saw each other only maybe four times. She was traveling all the time and I refused to leave Eternal Springs. This is my home, my place of business. I have family here, and friends — or at least, I thought I did."

His frosty gaze was not lost on me.

"We broke up after six months during an amicable and friendly phone call. She'd even rung me before coming to the island to see if I wanted to catch up and grab coffee. From the way it sounded, she was happily in a relationship."

"Wait a second — she was in a relationship?" I frowned. "None of the girls said anything about that."

"Maybe she wasn't — she didn't say either way," Mason said quickly. "Don't take my word on it. All I meant was that she sounded friendly and happy. I agreed to meet up with her but never got the chance. We were going to get coffee today."

"I'm really sorry, Mason," I said, softer. It wasn't until the phrase had slipped out that I realized my sympathies were already with him. For the second time today I'd approached someone thinking them a killer only to find myself upended and surprised by their side of the story. "But still, that doesn't explain —."

"— why I was out and about yesterday morning?" He gave a dry smile. "I have been over Mary for years. I've dated people after her. You have to understand, I'm unattached, but I'm also interested in someone."

"Oh?"

Mason gave a dry laugh. "You're not getting it. You, Evian. I'm interested in you. Haven't you noticed I tend to have a morning walk about the time you go to work every day? I know it sounds a little weird, but I swear I was just looking for a chance to run into you."

"Run into me?"

"A few weeks ago I walked to grab coffee. I came back from the shop and ran into you and we chatted for a few minutes," he said with a shrug. "You made me laugh. It's been a long time since someone made me laugh. I didn't forget that."

I knew the exact date he meant. It was the same day I'd noticed the curves of his arms and the flatness of his abs. The way his low, husky laugh warmed my insides and the way I got little butterflies every morning after when our paths seemed to accidentally cross.

"I figured I'd walked to get coffee anyway, why not chance a quick hello with you while I was at it?" He shrugged. "There was a pattern, see. My days were always a little bit brighter when I ran into you. So, I'm sorry, but there you have it."

"But it was raining!"

"It wasn't raining when I went to get coffee," he said. "You forget — you were an hour late to work. I walked down to get coffee and then the downpour hit. I waited at the shop for, like, an hour for it to pass, but eventually I had to get back home and to work. That's why I was jogging out there — trying to make it to work on time during the storm. Imagine my surprise when I ran into you even though it was an hour later than the normal time our paths crossed."

"You saw me in trouble ... ."

"So I came over to help. Look, Evian." Mason stepped around the counter. He left enough distance between us so that it wasn't intimidating, but there was no ambivalence in the way his eyes darkened as his gaze met mine. "You're funny, you're nice and of course you're beautiful. I'd be an idiot not to notice what's right in front of me."

"But Mason, the timing —."

"What about timing?" he interrupted. "I'm truly sorry that Mary is dead. I didn't tell you about my relationship with her because, well, first you're not the police. Sorry, but I didn't think you had any business knowing of my personal relationships with the deceased. Second, I'm interested in you. If ever the time came when you asked about dating history, I would have told you. I swear."

In the back of my mind, I heard Abigail's voice: *He's buttering you up, Evian. Why on earth would he ever chase after someone like you? Look at that bump on your nose, Evian. You wouldn't understand beauty pageants, Evian.*

I tried to push Abigail out, but she was still there, mouthing off in the back of my mind. The truth was that it was just too difficult to separate fact from fiction. Between the lies and twisted truths surrounding the murder investigation, coupled with the strange and new fascination I felt toward the island's mechanic, I was swimming in misgivings and uncertainties.

"Mason, I just think the timing for us isn't right. I'm trying to find out what happened to Mary, and —."

"— you don't want to have feelings for someone you consider a suspect." He spoke evenly, sadly. "I understand. I'm sorry to hear it, but I get it. Well, if it makes you feel better, I won't pursue you. Heck, I won't even get coffee at the same time anymore. Oh, and your scooter will be ready in a few days. I had to order a part from the mainland. It should be here tomorrow. Sorry about the delay."

"Mason ... ."

He raised an eyebrow, waiting for me to say more. After a

long moment, when I couldn't think up the proper words to explain myself, he gave a weary sigh.

"See you around, Evian," he said, and walked away from me to the golf cart.

I stood frozen in place, shocked by how much hurt I felt from his sudden burst of coldness, the resigned disinterest that he'd forced over the layer of warmth and humor that had drawn me to him in recent weeks.

"Hey, is that you, Evian?" Zola's voice startled me as she called from behind. "Oh, that's right. I heard your scooter got busted up. Got a minute? I hear you got a sludge monster eating your plants."

I chanced one more look at Mason, but he pretended valiantly that he hadn't heard. He continued tinkering away at the golf cart despite his shoulders inching up with tension.

"Yeah, sure," I told Zola, spinning on my heel and stepping through the still-open door of the front office. "Thanks for offering to help. I thought we'd better fix it before Paul has a cow."

"A toad having a cow," Zola cackled. "Funny."

"It's nice of you to help me out," I said. "Did Kenna bribe you?"

"Absolutely."

Eleven

"So, what do you get?" I asked as Zola scrounged around the flower bed in mud up to her elbows. "You know, for calling a truce to help me out."

"I've been hired to do all the arrangements for the beauty contest."

"It's a pageant."

"Whatever. I'll probably do them for Mary's funeral, too."

"That's morbid," I said. "Have fun with it. Say, what do you think about her death?"

"Isn't the whole purpose of me being here to get you to stop asking questions about that?"

"Whoa, whoa. Who said anything about stopping? I'm just supposed to be discreet."

"Yeah, okay. See how much Kenna appreciates that."

"Why's she not getting on Skye's case? She's asking around too."

"Yeah, but that's her job. Also, people are annoyed with you because Skye's been talking to them first."

I strolled over and sat on the front steps. As she worked, I watched her hands and knees get muddier and muddier, and noticed an ugly sort of scent that seemed to expand the more she turned up dirt. "What is wrong with my garden?"

"I don't know." Zola sat back crossly on her heels and wiped her hands on a pair of filthy jeans. "What the heck did you do to it? I've never seen this before. It's disgusting."

"My flowers are all turning to sludge."

"Everything's turning to sludge. Even the grass will be rotten soon. What are you doing home, anyway? Don't you work?"

"Wednesdays are my day off!" I said. "You'd know that if you listened to my show."

"Nobody listens to the show except a few creepy old guys and that one lady who somehow likes the nonstop calypso music."

"Well, I work weekends, so I make Leonard handle Wednesdays. Say, I think Bertha's watching," I said. "She'll be here in a second."

The whole time Zola had been working, my neighbor had been peering conspicuously out of her side window. Bertha liked to think she was the sneaky neighborhood gossip, but in reality there was nothing sneaky about her, nor did she know a thing about what anyone was doing. She was the worst neighborhood gossip I'd ever known. Most of the time, she just made stuff up if she didn't have anything to talk about.

"Well, what do we have here?" Bertha crept up to my gate and wrinkled her nose. "Smells horrible!"

"Sure does," I said cheerfully. Sometimes Bertha fed Paul if I couldn't make it home in time for lunch, so I did my best to keep her on my good side. "That's why Zola's here."

"Finally. It's about time you got someone who knows about flowers over here," Bertha said. Someone needed to tell her that gossiping often happened when the subject of the conversation wasn't directly before her. "What'd Evian do to her yard to make it so nasty?"

"I don't know. It's very bizarre." Zola had plunged her arms back into the flowerbed and was digging up the roots of something that had wilted. "Whatever it is seems to be rising to the surface from below. Something underground somehow."

"So it's not my fault?" I asked hopefully. "Could just be the dirt?"

"Dirt doesn't just turn into sludge," Zola said, dashing my hopes. "I don't know what you put in here — did you buy any cheap fertilizer?"

"Nada. I don't really do much of anything to my garden."

"Well, it's probably something you did unknowingly because it's isolated to your yard." Zola stood, glancing at the sky in the distance. The afternoon sun had begun to wane. Quite some time had passed without either of us realizing it. The oncoming darkness reminded me that we had a full moon this week — always a fun time for a water witch. "I have to get to the shop and get to work on funeral preparations. I'll ... . I don't know, I guess I'll look into this more tomorrow. I have some research to do first."

"Research quickly," Bertha said, thumbing over her shoulder toward the white picket fence that divided our properties. "I think her sludge is sliding over to my side of things and starting to swallow my raspberries. I don't appreciate that."

"I'd think not." Zola nodded toward my neighbor. "Let me take a few samples from around here that I can process back at the shop. Do you have a jar or something?"

I buzzed in the house, flustered as I looked for an empty jar. There was just one of me, and I wasn't a huge cook, so I didn't keep many supplies on hand.

Give her a cup, Paul said. *She can scoop dirt in there.*

I reached up for a spare margarita glass and pulled it down, then rushed outside to hand it over. "Here."

Zola gave me a strange look. I shrugged and she took the glass and dropped a pile of slop into it.

"Thanks, I guess," she said. "This should do. But if anyone sees me walking around holding a margarita glass of mud they'll think I'm nuts."

"Oh, honey," Bertha said, slapping her thigh. "Everyone already thinks y'all are nuts. The other two of you, as well. There must've been something funny about that convent they kept you in."

Someone — I don't remember who'd started the rumor — had explained that the magical school to which the four of us belonged had been a school for aspiring nuns. So, not only were we the odd four girls with a history nobody quite understood, but they all thought we'd been nuns-in-training until something went wrong. No wonder I hadn't had a date in years.

"Yeah, must have been," Zola said, standing. "Don't water your plants until I figure out what's going on — it's wet enough underground to drown most of them already."

I nodded my thanks. "Do you need a shower or something before you go?"

Zola glanced at her filthy jeans, her mud-streaked arms and the dark splotches on her shirt. "Nah. Part of the uniform. Anyway, I kept up my part of the deal, Evian, so ... ."

"I know," I said. "I'll keep up mine. I'll try to. But let me remind you that you haven't exactly fixed the problem yet, so I'm not going to stop asking questions."

"Asking questions about what?" Bertha wedged her nose tighter into the conversation. "This is that girl's murder y'all are talking about, isn't it?"

"We're not supposed to be talking about anything at all," Zola grimaced. "Isn't that right, Evian?"

"Fine," I muttered. "Thanks for your help. Let me know when you figure out what I need to do with these plants."

"I don't know that this is my area of expertise," Zola said, heading down the front walk with a mud margarita. "I don't know what's attacking your plants, Evian, but it's not looking good."

Twelve

The evening was already on the horizon so I decided to continue most of the intense sleuthing another day. The business with Zola had taken a few hours longer than I'd thought, and even though she hadn't been able to completely solve my problems, I hesitated to irk Kenna again so soon.

Bertha finally left sometime after Zola, realizing there probably wouldn't be much more gossip with just me and Paul. She wasn't aware that Paul was my familiar and could "talk" to me in his own way. Mostly, she just thought I was a weirdo who let her pet toad sit in margaritas like hot tubs.

Paul was just easing out of said tub. He gave a burp that told me he'd swallowed more than his fair share of the bathwater and gave a few clumsy hops toward me.

"Are you drunk?" I asked, looking up from the couch. "I thought I told you not to drink more than you could handle."

Nooope, Paul said, but even his thoughts were slurred.

I flicked my eyes back to the television and ignored Paul as he aimed a leap for my shoulder, missed, and ended up in my lap. "Paul."

"It's genocide out there," Paul said. "All the plants are dying. That's my home."

"You're a spoiled old toad who lives in a house and eat bon bons. You have a human at your beck and call. Don't pretend to be all nature-loving on me — you hate to get your feet dirty."

They're all dying, he moped. *If you don't find out what's happening, everything will die.*

"It's only my yard so far! I don't know why I've been the target." I pondered that for a moment, wondering why, indeed, it was only my yard. Normally I'd suspect a prank from one of the other witches, but because two of the three were involved in fixing the problem, they couldn't be behind the sludge in my yard. I might suspect Skye was using it to distract me from the case, but her specialty involved air, not dirt or water.

"You know what? Maybe it's not only my yard. Maybe it's affecting everything else." I stood up abruptly, sending Paul flying across the room. "Maybe we just can't see it."

Paul stuck to the metal part of a floor lamp and scowled at me. *Sure, go do more detective work. Who do you think you are, Nancy Drew?*

"If only I were as cool as Nancy Drew." I shrugged on a sweater. The sun had just dipped past the horizon and the chill would come on quickly. "I'm going for a walk — don't wait up for me. In fact, why don't you hop in bed and sleep things off?"

Sleep what off? Paul asked, his eyes unfocused as he looked at me. *Yeah, okay. I'll go to bed.*

I offered an olive branch by extending a hand and letting Paul jump into my palm. His bed was in the small porch area, so he had a nice breeze to keep him cool. Apparently he ran warmer than most toads because he complained his feet got hot when he slept inside, though that might have been due to the fact that I tucked him in with a miniature down comforter. Kenna liked to say I needed to cut the umbilical cord with Paul. On days like today, I tended to see her point.

I settled him into the doll-sized bathtub that he preferred for sleeping and watched as he hunkered down.

When I was sure he was settled for the night, I let myself out of the front porch and made my way down the sidewalk. Bertha was watching from the window, so I made a big show of waving in her direction before heading toward Coconuts. I'd purposely orchestrated my route so she'd think I was heading down for another drink (she probably thought I was the one who bathed in margaritas). It was better she thought I was headed to the bar than finding out my real itinerary: a night walk through Cottonmouth Copse.

Most people wouldn't dream of walking through a forest at night. And *especially* not the day after a murder had occurred. But I knew the forest better than most, and though it wasn't my favorite place, I needed information.

I made a hard turn to the left and split from the main path once I was out of Bertha's sight. A smaller footpath led the way from behind my house, through a series of fields, until the trees loomed ahead of me.

The trees of Cottonmouth Copse could talk. These particular varieties weren't exactly known for their friendliness, but they *were* known for their gossip. I figured it wouldn't hurt to wander among them, to listen to the whispers and sift through the information. There was a chance they'd know who — or what — had become intent on killing my plants.

"Haven't gotten a new haircut yet, *hmm?*" Agatha, one of the trees, shouted as I entered the shadowy woods. "You've had the same *'do* since the nineties."

Have I mentioned these trees thrive on sarcasm? Trees and cats. When the incident at our school sent witches fleeing to the mainland, many of their familiars had been lost and abandoned. Some of them could still be found slinking through the underbrush while the trees cackled at us from above.

"Your shirt's on backward," one of the oaks said, then gave a childish cackle. "Made ya look."

"I didn't look," I said. "The joke doesn't work if I don't fall for it."

That shut up at least one of the trees. The rest continued to mumble and groan as I entered beneath their curved boughs, the silence dampening and all-consuming, the shadows deep and heavy. By the time I'd reached the center of the copse, all I heard was the creaking of branches swaying in the wind and the scratch of dry leaves as they clashed against one another.

Apparently the sarcasm gene hadn't traveled this far because the voices were silent — until one spoke in a deep, rumbling sort of echo, a sound that radiated from the depth of its roots.

"What have you brought on us?" The tree intoned. "And why have you come into our midst?"

"What have I brought on you?" I asked, glancing at my feet to make sure I wasn't stepping on any tender roots. "I came to ask you questions. I didn't bring anything on you."

"You did, years ago," he said. "If it weren't for you ... we would not be dying."

"Dying? You're dying? You all seem pretty chipper, actually. Especially Agatha."

"It takes longer for the blackness to reach our core. We are trees with roots that go deep, with years of protection. Not like your little daisies and grasses that shudder at one touch of the shadow and shrivel."

"So you feel it too? That sludge?"

"Of course — and soon it will spread. From your yard,

from the depths of the ground, to all. The island will cease to produce living plants of any sort if you don't stop the progression."

"How do I stop it? What *is* it? I just thought I had a black thumb."

"You do have a black thumb, but that's not the reason your plants are dying." The tree swayed closer to me. "It's to do with the incident that opened the portal years ago."

"Are you saying this sludge, or whatever it is, came from the open gate?"

"Yes."

I raised a hand, scratched at my forehead as I stalled, thinking. "But how? We are watching the portal. There's not a huge mudslide pouring out of it. We might have a reputation for being oblivious, but we would've noticed *that*."

"Whatever is causing the problem is not from this realm," the tree said. "It feeds on life and magic, and leaves behind death and destruction and decay. The more it kills, the stronger it grows."

I shuddered. The tree sensed my movement because he bent his branches in a way that reflected a nod.

"Indeed," he said. "It is terrifying. Now, go, guardian of the portal, and fix the mess you and the others have made."

"The portal opening wasn't my fault!" I argued. "All four of us were on duty the night of the incident. All of us should have been watching it, and instead ... ."

"Go," he commanded. "Swiftly!"

I stopped making excuses, turned, and made a quick exit. The trees had begun to creak louder, as if itching to get their hands on the witch who'd started this mess.

"Get a haircut!" Agatha yelled as I stumbled back under the moonlight. "Try a new style. Have one of them beauty pageant ladies to give you a makeover!"

"And while you're at it," a second male tree shouted, "send

some of the ladies this way. We don't see much in the way of outsiders anymore. Something about people saying this place is dangerous."

"Creep," I muttered. "You just want to ogle beautiful women."

"Hey, I might be a tree, but I'm still a male," he said, and cackled. "Get out of here, witch. And take the thing that's out to kill us with you. If we die, you die. We're taking you down with us."

Another shudder. I picked up the pace and hurried back down the path, retracing my steps. When I re-emerged onto the main road, I instinctively turned toward home, and then caught myself.

It was still early enough to swing by the Beauty Cottage. While I was out and about, I could grab the names of the vendors who had been scheduled to show up the morning of Mary's murder. I couldn't do much else tonight, and Paul was sleeping off his bath at home. With no real technology on the island, I'd be stuck watching a DVD of *Boy Meets World* because I was feeling too lazy to pop it out of the machine and change it for something new.

Billie Jo answered the door two seconds after I knocked, and I wondered if she'd been appointed as the official greeter. Or, maybe she'd given the title to herself because she was the only one familiar with the locals. Frankly, after a murder on the premises, I wouldn't want to be the first line of defense between the outside world and the Beauty Cottage, but I didn't say that to her.

"Hey there, Billie," I said. "I have a question for you. Is there any chance you have a list of the vendors who were supposed to be here yesterday morning?"

"Oh, um, sure," she said. "Why? Did you see something you wanted to buy?"

"Something like that," I said, and inched my way into the

house as Billie Jo spun on her heel and marched toward the dining room. "Let's see, I think Edwin left something around here — or sent an itinerary over. Someone coordinates these things, but not me."

"Don't rush, I don't mind waiting. Maybe one of the other girls knows where it might be?"

"Sure, sure," she said distractedly. "Let me go ask Sandy. She even folds her underwear, sweet thing. She's the most organized of all of us."

"Thanks. I appreciate that."

I waited in the dining area where she'd left me, but after five minutes had passed I wondered if Billie Jo had forgotten all about me. I strolled through the kitchen and found a surprising hodge-podge of liquids. There was an odd dichotomy that divided the kitchen between healthy beverages and alcohol. On one counter sat all the fixings for green smoothies: protein powder, fresh fruit, vegetables, spinach (super gross) and kale (even worse). The other half of the room had been taken over by a mixture of liquor and wine bottles. After a quick glimpse, I found the refrigerator nearly empty. Apparently these girls survived on fruit smoothies for breakfast and cosmopolitans for dinner.

"Oh, sorry." Tarryn, Mary's former competition, strolled into the kitchen and stopped short. "I didn't know you were in here. I'll come back."

"Just ignore me! I'm waiting for Billie Jo." I waved a hand and gestured for her to take over. "Guess I'm just a bit nosy."

"Guess you are," she said. "Otherwise you wouldn't be asking around about Mary so much."

I was surprised by the barbed comment because she'd seemed so sweet in our previous interview. Sure, I'd detected a hint of strength to her and a layer of sass hidden behind the soft, southern exterior, but I hadn't suspected her to be confrontational.

"I'm just trying to figure out what happened to Mary," I said. "I found the body, and —."

"So what?" Tarryn asked, reaching into the fridge and pulling out a gallon of chocolate milk. She didn't offer me any as she poured herself a glass. "You found her body. Big deal — she wasn't a friend to you like she was to us. You were in the right place at the right time."

"I'd call it the wrong place at the wrong time," I said. "I wasn't exactly excited to find a woman's body on my way to work. Sort of a day dampener, don't you think?"

My attempt at humor didn't work on Tarryn. She scowled. "You think it's funny?"

"No, it's, like, you know, cops and their black humor. It's meant to help deal with the situation."

"But you're not a cop."

"No, but ... ." I hesitated. "Look, Tarryn, I'm really sorry for your loss. I'm only trying to help Mary."

"She's dead. How does this help her?"

"She deserves justice! She was killed — *murdered*," I said. "Hopefully this will help with closure for her family. They'll want to know who is responsible for their friend, sister, daughter's death. Mary was all of those things."

"Yeah, and you're a pretty good actress." Tarryn leaned against the counter. "Normally I'd believe you, but I think you're trying to get ratings for your show."

My cheeks flamed. There was some truth to her accusations, but that wasn't the only reason I was running myself through the wringer in the hunt for Mary's killer. I knew it, but Tarryn didn't. "I can see how you'd think that, but it's not true. Look, I invited you onto the show before Mary died. It's just part of the business — the pageant is a big deal. The offer is still open if you want to come on the air."

Tarryn paused, halfway through her glass of milk. "Okay."

"Okay, what?" I asked. "Okay you'll come on?"

"Fine," she said. "But only to talk about Mary and pay respects. It's not about you or your stupid ratings. And you can't ask any questions about the pageant."

"Absolutely," I agreed. "I won't ask a thing you don't want to talk about. Just give me a list of topics to avoid."

"No. It won't be a long interview — it's not about *me*; it's about Mary. She's gone, but she has friends left behind, and we haven't forgotten her."

"That's very nice of you."

"Not all of us think the *show should go on*," she said with a snap, and I wondered if she'd had a glass of wine before the chocolate milk. She seemed almost a different person than the one I'd interviewed the day before. "A senseless murder and here we all are, prancing around in our bathing suits and singing and dancing despite it all. Seems disrespectful, doesn't it?"

"Is it what Mary would have wanted?"

"I don't know!" Tarryn slammed her glass down on the counter. "Nobody does. Because she's dead."

"Here you ... oh, *sorry*." Billie Jo flounced into the room, stopping when she saw Tarryn glaring at me. "I'll come back."

"No. Stay," Tarryn said. "I'm leaving."

Billie Jo raised her eyebrows as Tarryn stormed out of the room. "She's taking Mary's death really hard. I swear she's a sweet girl — this isn't like her."

"I understand. Were they friends?"

Billie Jo shrugged. "Who knows? I suppose they were, but it wasn't as if they were the best of friends. At least not that I knew of. Like I told you before, we're pretty much all friendly with one another."

"Is that the list?" I extended a hand and reached for the paper Billie Jo had begun to hand me. "May I see it?"

"Yeah, of course." She pushed it forward and stood by my shoulder. "The three that are highlighted in yellow are the vendors who showed up and were sent away the morning of Mary's ... well, the morning she died."

"Thank you so much. This is really helpful," I said, and wondered if I'd finally stumbled across something that Skye hadn't. "Do you know if any of them are still in town?"

Billie Jo shrugged. "Maybe Edwin will know, but I doubt it. He doesn't pay attention except for the big stuff. Actually, Carl might know — he paid attention to all of that beauty stuff for Mary."

"Are you familiar with any of them?" I glanced over the names listed there. LOREEN, ELEMENTAL BEAUTY and NATURAL INSTINCTS all printed in big block letters. "Have you used their products before? Or met with the reps?"

"Loreen is fancy and too expensive," Billie Jo said, "which is why all the girls love their samples. It's about the only thing we can afford from them. Except for Mary — I think she got free stuff from them all the time because she won, of course."

I filed that away and pointed at the next one.

"Elemental Beauty is middle of the road," she said with a shrug. "We all buy plenty of their stuff. I think they're starting a line of fancy products and had given Mary some as a trial package, but I don't know for sure. I know she had a horrible reaction to something — face cream, I think — but I don't know whose it was. Natural Instincts is basically the hippie line. You know, plant and organic and gluten free and whatever." She shrugged. "I might buy it, but again ... costly."

"Thank you so much for this," I said. "I really appreciate —."

Billie Jo stiffened. "Do you hear the music? We're all going to practice our waves. You can stay if you want, but you'll probably be bored. Shall I show you out?"

Before I could answer, I found myself edged onto the front steps as the door lock clicked shut behind me.

"Appreciate it," I said. "Bye."

The sound of music filled the house. I turned toward the main road and began a leisurely stroll home. The night was cool but not cold, the breeze refreshing and crisp. As I tugged my sweater closer to me, I happened to glance over my shoulder.

I halted, my heart pounding as I caught sight of a face in the upstairs window of the cottage. A bedroom, no doubt, with the glow illuminating a figure from behind.

Tarryn.

She waited a second longer, watching me, before she turned and disappeared from the window. It wasn't exactly threatening, but for the rest of the walk home I felt the creepy sensation of eyes burning holes in my back.

It wasn't until I finally climbed into bed dressed in fresh pajamas and warm from my shower that I realized I wasn't sure if she'd ever confirmed our interview for the next morning. She'd agreed, then stormed off. I guess it would be an on-air surprise for everyone.

Thirteen

"What do you mean you think you might have an interview?" Leonard said, fumbling with the schedule. "You either have one or you don't."

"It's complicated!" I'd shuffled into the studio a few minutes before the show was scheduled to begin. "If she shows up, send her in here. That's all I'm saying."

I'd waited until the last possible second to tell Leonard about the potential interview with Tarryn. A part of me had hoped she'd show up early and I wouldn't have to come up with an awkward explanation for what had happened last night, but that hadn't panned out.

"I have programming that needs following," Leonard shouted. "You can't just maybe disrupt the schedule for the day. I mean sure, if you'd secured an actual interview we could slot her in. But this isn't amateur hour, we're Hex 66.6!"

"Yeah, and how many people tune in daily?" I raised my eyebrows and stared at Leonard. "I'm sure if Tarryn shows up it'll be great for ratings. And nobody will miss the weather update that we're skipping to fit her in. Anyway, it's no use getting our undies in a bunch over something that might not ... *Tarryn!*"

"My name's Leonard," he said. "And you shouldn't talk to your employees like that. If you want to —."

"Leonard." I coughed as Tarryn entered the room behind him, looking tentative, as if she wasn't sure whether she'd arrived in the right place. "Our guest is here."

"Oh, *Tarryn!*" Leonard put a huge, cheesy grin on his face as he turned around and reached for her hand. His smile faded as he realized a more somber note was in order. "I am so sorry for your loss. From all I've heard, Mary was an amazing woman."

"She was." Tarryn looked demure in a slim black dress that swished just above her knees. The lace sleeves and high neckline gave off a slight *Breakfast at Tiffany's* vibe. "Thanks for having me on today."

I was so shaken by the switch in personality from last night that I couldn't find the proper response.

Finally, Leonard stepped in for me. "Of course — we appreciate you coming down to the station to chat with us. It must be hard with everyone expecting you to act as if all is normal and go on with the pageant."

Both Tarryn and I gave him a look of surprise. I hadn't known Leonard could display normal human emotions, let alone a sense of sympathy — everything he said seemed to hover around increasing ratings. Either I'd underestimated him or he was very good at faking sympathy.

"It is hard," she said. "And it's frustrating. The world thinks we should just move on when many of us are dealing with the death of a close friend."

"Now, let's get you seated so we can get some of this on air," Leonard said, returning to his usual self. "The public needs to hear your message."

While Leonard closed the room and entered the booth

next to us, I sat in front of the microphone and helped Tarryn get situated with hers.

"I'm sorry if I upset you last night," I said. "I shouldn't have come around asking questions."

"No, I'm sorry I reacted like I did. It's an emotional time," she said flatly. "I hope you understand."

Though I understood her words, I couldn't quite figure out Tarryn Southland. Sometimes she seemed overwhelmed with emotion — anger and sadness and frustration — and other times she seemed borderline emotionless.

"When the light blinks, it means we're on air," I quickly explained. "I won't ask you any hard-hitting questions, but if anything makes you uncomfortable just give me the signal and we'll move onto something else."

She gave a nod. That was followed shortly by a few hand gestures from Leonard and then the light flicked on.

"Good morning, Eternal Springs," I said. "Here with your break from calypso music this is Evian Brooks with a special guest. Unfortunately, her visit is tinged with tragedy. Most of you will know her name, so without further ado, let us welcome Tarryn Southland to Hex 66.6!"

"Hi, Evian," Tarryn spoke into the mic with a velvety voice. "Thank you for having me here today."

"Of course. I'm sorry the circumstances couldn't be better," I said, refraining to add that she'd turned me down flat for an interview before Mary had been murdered. "Welcome to the show. Can you start by telling us a little about yourself and your friendship with Mary?"

"Well, I'd prefer not to talk about myself," she said and, though her voice was smooth, her eyes shot daggers at me. "But Mary, certainly. I knew her first as Marilyn from New Jersey," she said with a soft laugh. "We were polar opposites in the beauty pageant circuit. I was the rural southern gal while she was the blond jersey girl with a bit of sass to her — but not too much. She was the sweetest thing."

"From what I hear, none of the contestants have a bad word to say about her."

"No, I can't think of anyone who might have anything negative to say. And that's rare for a girl who won fifty-nine pageants." Tarryn looked into the distance and gave a sad smile. "But that's the type of person she was. She truly had a heart of gold."

"Can you share any memories of the times the two of you were on pageant tours?"

Tarryn gave a slight nod. "Well, one time, we were in the middle of nowhere Minnesota, competing at some pageant in the dead cold of winter. Around three in the morning we were so starved because our takeout had never arrived that we decided to borrow the coordinator's car without him knowing."

"Uh-oh," I said with a grin. "He can't have been happy about that."

She laughed. "Not at all. It was icy and snowy, and I'll let you figure out how that ended up. Neither of us knew how to drive well in those conditions, and we landed halfway into a snowbank. The whole time we were waiting for the tow truck to pull us out we huddled together for warmth. From then on out, no matter who won which pageant, we didn't care. We were in it together, you know?"

"Of course. Thanks for sharing that memory," I said, and then threw her another softball question.

So far, so good.

We chatted for a good ten-minute segment and reminisced over Mary's finest moments, her greatest wins and the loss that her death brought the community.

Finally, I hit the button to pause, and the stupid calypso tune completely ruined the tender moment we'd ended on.

"Sorry about that," I said, flinching at the music. "Something is up with the station, and it's stuck on this track. It's not fitting for the moment, I know."

She stretched. "I have to be heading out after this, so maybe we can say our goodbyes on air?"

"Absolutely. Say, Tarryn ... ." I moved the mic so it was just the two of us talking. "I have a question for you — I know you don't think I should be looking into the murder, but I swear I'm doing it to help Mary. I haven't even reported on the story save for interviewing you! Not to mention, Skye, the newspaper reporter, has a full spread by now. More news will leak out every day — it's going to be impossible to keep things quiet."

"That doesn't make the problem any better," she said. "I really dislike when people use horrific things to promote themselves."

I sighed. "Maybe you can tell me a bit about the vendors who were at the cottage that morning. Billie Jo gave me a list, and I wanted to ask if they'd seen anything."

Tarryn bit her lip, debating. "I don't know much about them. I don't visit the vendors much because I get most of their products free anyway. The top three or so girls in each pageant have enough makeup to last a lifetime with all the freebie packs we receive."

I pushed the list toward her. "Anything suspicious about any of these?"

She frowned. "Loreen is just ridiculously expensive. Natural Instincts is all-natural stuff. I like their products, but I think they're also selling a load of crock with their marketing. This one ... ." she tapped on Elemental Beauty. "Mary was furious with them."

"Why?"

"Well, they are trying to make this new line of high-end skin care and they sent her a sample to try out," she said. "It gave her hives. The stuff is horrible — I wouldn't have blamed her if she gave them a terrible review. Mary had hundreds of thousands of followers on social media. None of them would've bought the product after a scathing review from her. She never says anything bad about anyone."

I blinked, unwilling to believe my luck. "Did she tell them that?"

"Of course not."

"But that didn't mean someone couldn't have found out," I said. "Surely Carl knew of her experience, or some of the girls."

"Maybe, but ... they wouldn't have killed her over it."

"Carl and the girls — no. But what about someone from Elemental Beauty? It might have crippled their business. Plus, a representative was scheduled to be at the Beauty Cottage during the time Mary died. Motive and opportunity are both there."

Tarryn cocked her head to the side, but we didn't get to finish the conversation because the on-air light blinked again.

"We're back," I said. "Unfortunately, it's time to say goodbye to our guest, Tarryn Southland. Any last parting words, Tarryn?"

"Sure," she said, purring into the microphone. "I just want to send my condolences to Mary's family and all who were close to her."

"Of course, and that's —."

"And that I wish people would stop exploiting her murder to raise their show's ratings," she said, her eyes darkening as she stared at me. "Lastly, for anyone using Elemental Beauty products, I recommend you stop at once."

I gestured wildly for Leonard to cut back to music, but he was too stunned to move. There was nothing I could do except halfheartedly attempt to interrupt Tarryn. That was a fine line, however, since cutting her off completely would look incredibly rude and paint me in a horrible light.

"Their new line is a ruse, and it will make your skin break out in hives," Tarryn finished. "There, I think that's all. Thanks for your time, Evian."

She stood and stormed out of the studio.

Finally, after a horrid three seconds of dead air, Leonard flailed to hit the button.

Calypso music filled the airwaves once more.

Fourteen

"Ratings are through the charts!" Leonard yelled into the phone the second I picked up my landline. "I've been replaying your segment with Tarryn on a loop and every time we pick up more listeners. It's as if people want to hear you get *wrecked*!"

"I didn't get wrecked by her," I said. "She just expressed her opinions."

"Uh, sure. Whatever you want to call it. Each time around we get more listeners. I'll bet you half the island has heard this segment, and the other half is talking about it. We're going to be the number one show in Eternal Springs!"

"I don't know *how* we could beat Mitzi's show."

"But people actually want to listen to us this time. They're not just flicking the radio on because there's no other option and they're forced to listen to HEX 66.6."

"Gee whiz. Exciting."

"We need more conflict on the show. I want to get some controversial guests. Maybe I can get two of the beauty contestants onto the show to really rip into one another. You know, air all that dirty laundry for the public to hear?"

"I don't really think that's the best way to go about drumming up listeners."

"But the drama?"

"Why can't we report on the weather and traffic and important issues? Mary's murder is an important issue. That's why I invited Tarryn on in the first place."

"Screw important, I want the cat fights! Did you meet anyone at the Beauty Cottage who seemed inclined to put up a good fight? Maybe one of the more jealous gals or ... oh, I know! Someone who really hated Tarryn?"

"None of them seem to hate each other at all. In fact, they're friends," I told Leonard. "You're frustrating. Bye."

"Don't you think it's odd?" The curious tone in his voice stopped me from hanging up

"What's odd?"

"That they're all so friendly." Leonard's question was surprisingly insightful. "I mean, I don't think of beauty pageants as Miss buddy-buddy girl-time. It's a competition! Women can get emotional."

"Watch your step, buddy."

"I'm not talking about any woman in particular," he said. "And I suppose guys could get emotional too in the same situation. Humans are competitive — they want to win, especially if there's a prize on the line. What's the prize for winning?"

"Ten thousand dollars and, of course, the intangible fame from taking first place."

"Exactly. Don't you think that could be a motive worth killing over?"

"I don't know. Ten grand is a lot of money, but not exactly a life-altering sum."

"No, but throw in the residuals from the fame, the free samples, the endorsement deals ... ." He paused to let his theories sink in. "And that's not the end of it — I mean, the emotional side of it. I'm not talking about women only — men feel competitive and envious. Jealousy is a strong motivator."

He did have a point. Male or female, beauty contestants or not, I'd rarely stepped into a house full of people and found that one-hundred percent of them liked one another. Surely some of them had been fibbing, even downright lying, about their feelings toward Mary. But *who*?

Had it been Tarryn, and was she now overcompensating to prove she'd been friends with the deceased? Or someone quieter like Billie Jo, who loved to be the center of attention — always answering the door and taking charge — but didn't have a trophy to her name?

I was still thinking when Leonard gave a disinterested yawn. His attention span waned at the slightest bit of dead air.

"Well, when you find out who had a bone to pick with Mary, invite her on the show, will you?" he suggested. "It'll be good for both of us. And you can't tell me one of them won't be coming forward what with all the attention Tarryn just got on air. They'll be clamoring to be interviewed by you, Evian. Take it and run with it. Might be the only chance you'll get."

"Gee, thanks."

"Bye. See you tomorrow. Stir up some trouble."

With those sage words, I hung up the phone and blew out a sigh of exasperation. I'd run home immediately after the show and told myself it was because I was respecting my deal with Kenna and Zola — and not because I didn't want to be seen in public after the fleecing I'd gotten from Tarryn.

I was deep into pretending I wasn't embarrassed. As I began looking for Paul, who had yet to surface since I'd returned home, I wondered if Tarryn was right. Was I exploiting people during a challenging time just to up show ratings?

"Where are you?" I muttered, as I knelt to check under the table. "Come out of your hiding spot, Paul. I'm in no mood."

It's my job, I told myself, still lost in thought as I scoured the rest of the house. Skye was doing the same thing. Heck, cops did a similar thing. They looked into crimes and sometimes had to report to the media. I was basically an untrained, uncertified cop who had zero qualifications. *Yeah, right.*

"Paul!" I shouted. "I give up. If you don't come out soon, I'll have you declared dead!"

A distinctly toad-like groan came from my room.

"Oh, no you didn't," I said. "What did I tell you about sleeping in my bed? Gross! I don't want toad germs all over my covers. No margarita baths for you for a month."

Paul croaked again, sounding genuinely in pain. I moved down the hall, more concerned with each step. It wasn't like Paul to revert to his native language. He considered himself much too posh to grunt around like the rest of his kind. He preferred bon bons and margaritas, after all.

"What's wrong?" I pulled the covers back to reveal Paul perched on a small, fluffy pink pillow that would definitely have to be tossed out now. Even as I found him, I began pulling the sheets off the bed and throwing them toward the hamper. "Why'd you come hide out in here?"

I saw it, he told me. *I saw the thing.*

"What thing?"

The thing that's been eating your plants. Devouring them. It's disgusting. Filthy and huge.

"What was it?"

I don't know. It looked like some gigantic slug!

"I don't mean to be rude, but you sound insane. Bertha stares out her window at this house all day long. Surely if there were a giant gastropod on my lawn she would've called the police. Or me! She'd at least call me!"

She couldn't see it. It's from the other realm.

"People can still see creatures from the other realm."

Some of them, yes, but this one ... . Paul shuddered. *I don't know what he — er, it —was. It shimmered. At one point, Bertha stared right at him. She didn't so much as flinch.*

"Well, where'd it go? I didn't see anything when I got home."

I didn't stick around to find out.

"Some giant sludge monster — invisible to the human eyes — is ruining my garden?" I raised my eyebrows. "You're sure."

It's an ugly, horrifying thing.

"Paul, I'm sorry, but I haven't heard of anything like this before. You have to admit it sounds bizarre."

It's more believable than all your plants suddenly just up and wilting. Zola couldn't figure out what was wrong with any of them, and she's an earth witch.

"Fine, fine," I said. "I'll go check. But for the record, I think you're still being paranoid. Not that I blame you. Having a murderer on the loose is enough to make even the bravest of us scared."

I'm not brave — I'm too pretty to be brave.

"Right. Now, hop off," I said. "Back to your own bed. Even if this sludge monster is real, it wouldn't come through our doors. Go on, I have to wash everything now."

Once I'd begun the process of bleaching my sheets, I returned downstairs to apologize to Paul. After all, he was my familiar, and hurting his feelings wouldn't get either of us anywhere. Who knew? Maybe he had seen something and was exaggerating. After all, the trees had hinted that the portal had opened and something was amiss.

My journey to the porch was interrupted when I found

three sets of legs stretched across the ottoman in front of my couch. Turning, I found Skye, Kenna and Zola sitting in my living room. Apparently they'd let themselves in and made themselves comfortable. Zola held a cup of tea while Skye had scored a soda from the fridge. Kenna sat with her arms crossed, fuming.

"Looks like I'm in trouble, huh?" I asked. "To what do I owe the honor of this visit?"

"You need a better guard dog," Skye said. "Paul let us walk right on by."

"I don't keep him for his guard capabilities." I sniffed, feeling defensive. "Paul is the sensitive type, anyway, and he's been having a rough day."

"I thought we had a deal." Kenna leaned forward on the couch. "I went through all this effort to wrangle Zola into helping you with your stupid plants, and what did you do? You drew more attention to the case than ever before. And now I'm stuck using Zola to do the flowers for the beauty pageant and the funeral, and you're not holding up your end of the bargain."

"You say that like it's a hardship," Zola shot back. "You know I have the best floral arrangements on the island. You're lucky I offered to help; otherwise Mrs. Maybell would have set you up with a bunch of dead roses again."

"Why are the two of you fighting?" Skye asked them. "We came here to gang up on Evian."

"Look, I didn't plan on Tarryn coming into the interview and reacting the way she did," I said. "She seemed genuinely upset, and I thought she only wanted to say a few kind words about Mary. That's within the scope of my job."

"So you didn't go around asking questions?" Kenna raised an eyebrow. "You didn't head over to the Beauty Cottage and pester the girls there until someone agreed to come on the show?"

"I didn't pester anyone."

"But you went over there," she persisted, "and you continued to ask questions. After we'd explicitly agreed you wouldn't do that."

"If we want to get technical, then Zola was supposed to solve the problem with my yard, or at least diagnose it!" I said. "So *technically*, nobody's end of the bargain has been upheld."

"It's not my fault I don't know what the heck you put in your dirt," Zola said. "Did you buy the cheapest fertilizer you could find or something? Or did Swoops lose control of his bowels again?"

"Swoops is fine," Skye said of her mischievous bat familiar. "Anyway, bat droppings are conducive to growing healthy plants. It's common knowledge."

"Not in his quantities," Zola muttered. "He smothers the poor plants."

"You know it's coming from the portal. It's nothing I or Swoops or anyone else did." I stepped further into the room and faced the three of them. "Actually, I was laying off the investigation. Instead, I was trying to find out why all my plants are dying and took a walk in the woods. Guess what the trees think?"

Zola bit her lip. "The trees are worried?"

"Well, most of them are still sarcastic, but the big one in the middle —."

"Charles?"

"I don't know his name, but sure, we can call him Charles." I met the other girls' gazes evenly. "He seems to think that something has escaped from the portal. Which never would have happened if you all had been paying attention thirteen years ago! We might all be off this island if that were the case!"

"Hey now," Kenna warned. "That wasn't my fault."

"It wasn't mine!" Zola chirped. "I was watching."

"We were all on duty," Skye said. "And I was paying attention, so it had to be one of you."

"Apparently we all agree to disagree," I said. "And if you came here to lecture me, you can head out. I have things to do. I have a monster to find, a murder to solve and a toad to comfort."

"What's wrong with Paul?" Zola's eyes narrowed. She's always had a fond spot for the toad, though she'd deny it if asked. "Is he ill?"

"Scared. He thinks he saw ... ." I cleared my throat, feeling ridiculous. "A giant slug."

"Bertha would've called the cops," Kenna scoffed. "She spies on you like a stalker. Lucky for her she didn't get a more interesting neighbor or she'd have a heart attack."

"Hey!" I snapped. "I think that was an insult. I'm not *that* boring."

"Good job; you learned to recognize an insult. That's the first step," Skye said. "*Bravo.*"

"Fine — I'm going," Kenna said. "You won't listen to reason anyway."

"What about the portal monster?" I asked. "Shouldn't we all find it together? We were all on duty the night things got busted open in the first place."

"Do you really expect us to believe Paul saw a sludge monster?" Kenna stood. "The toad is scared of his shadow. It was probably a branch waving in the dark."

"What else could it be?" Though I'd wondered the same thing, I felt the need to defend my toad's honor. "Zola hasn't seen anything like this before and the trees are talking about supernatural sludge, so I think we have to consider that something has slipped out of the portal. It's happened before."

"Well, whatever it is has a target on your back, not ours," Kenna pointed out. "Why's it affecting only your yard?"

"I don't know all the answers," I said. "I think we should look into it further."

"Sure. When you have proof that your toad isn't lying," Skye said, "then call us over and we'll rescue you from the giant slug."

I couldn't say I blamed them. It was a bit of a stretch to believe Paul's story about an invisible-to-humans monster that happened to pop up while I'd been away. Paul had probably panicked at being caught sleeping in my bed and made up the first story he thought of to avoid getting in trouble.

"Fine," I said. "I'll look around and let you know. Now, if you don't mind, I have work to do."

My three sister witches filed out of the room, depositing their mugs and cans and beverage supplies on the counter. I let them out and locked the door after them.

"Nobody believes you, Paul," I said to the toad, who was pretending to snore in his bed. "You have to admit, it's pretty weird."

You don't think I know it's weird? Of course I know I sound like a crazy old toad. But I know what I saw, Evian. Trust me.

I sighed. "Oddly enough, I don't have any better option. I don't know where to start: hunting paranormal monsters or tracking down a human killer?"

Good riddance to both. Paul shuddered. *I'm staying in bed.*

Fifteen

I opted for the murderer. Somehow, it seemed more appealing to track down a killer than a giant slug.

That's the very thought that had me concerned as I grabbed my purse and headed down the front steps. But the universe had a different idea. Apparently leaving my house wasn't on the agenda for today, seeing as I was continually interrupted with each consecutive effort.

"Evian!" Mason greeted me with a shy smile. His shoulders were slumped forward and a pinched look of discomfort tainted his otherwise friendly demeanor. "I thought I might find you here."

"It is my house, after all."

He gave a short laugh. "Yeah, well. I just came by to say, well ... ."

"Did you hear the segment on the radio?" I asked, shifting my weight on the front steps. "It's fine if you did. Come to make fun of me for it?"

"I'd never do that, Evian. I came to say I'm sorry for how things shook out."

"It's just part of the job."

"That's not the only reason I'm here."

I locked the door behind me, feigning disinterest. "Really? Sorry, but I'm running out somewhere, so I can't talk long."

He stepped closer. "Off to look for the Elemental Beauty vendor?"

Surprise registered on my face so quickly there was no chance of hiding it. "How'd you know?"

"I feel like I've gotten to know you pretty well over the last few weeks," he said with a grin. "I figured one little radio segment wouldn't stop you from investigating. If anything, I thought it might prompt you to look harder."

"Aren't you the next Sherlock?" I folded my arms across my chest, cautiously waiting. "Well? What about it?"

"I have it on good authority that the name of Elemental Beauty's vendor is Darren Whiting. He was the one scheduled for the day Mary was murdered."

"How'd you get that information?"

"Hanging out at the coffee shop during what might be the most gossip-filled week of Eternal Springs's history has its pros."

"Fair enough." I hesitated. "And do you know where this Darren Whiting might be?"

His eyes twinkled, and we both knew he had me right in his crosshairs. "There's a catch. I also have a request."

"What do you want from me?" I raised an eyebrow. "I already bring my scooter to you at least seven times a year. Any more and I'll go broke."

"This isn't of the professional variety," he said. "In fact, it's quite personal. I'd like you to agree to have dinner with me."

"We just had tacos the other day. Sort of."

"If I remember correctly, *you* had tacos. And you hadn't planned to meet me there. That was a lucky coincidence."

"Either way, consider dinner had."

Mason stepped forward to close the gap between us.

"Come on, Evian. You don't really think I'm responsible for Mary's death, do you?"

I shifted further away. "I thought you were upset with me for considering it."

"I was upset — I am upset. Wouldn't it upset you if someone — especially someone you thought a friend — accused you of murder?"

"I suppose," I said uneasily. "But you have to look at things from my point of view, too. We're friends, sort of, but I don't know you that well. I'm trying to be objective and follow the facts."

"I understand, and that's why I'm here with this awkward sort of apology," he said. "Or shall we call it a truce?"

"I just feel —."

"Let me guess. You feel uncomfortable agreeing to anything because the murderer is not locked up yet. So long as the killer's still free, you have to keep your eye out and not let anything — or anyone — get in your way."

I shrugged. "I'm sorry."

"I can work with that. I'll trade you information if you agree to a date with me. I won't redeem the date card until this case is closed." He hesitated, then scowled. "I'm sorry, that came out wrong. I'm not blackmailing you, Evian. That sounded stupid. Darren Whiting is on his way to the ferry as we speak. There, now you have it. That's all I know, and there's no catch."

"Thank you," I said, oddly touched that he'd come to freely offer the information.

Unless ... he was guilty, and this was his way of sending me on a goose chase. *Ugh*.

"I'm going to head out now," he said. "But consider the offer. I swear to you, Evian, I told you the truth. I had nothing to do with Mary's murder."

"I-I think I believe you." As soon as the words left my

mouth his face fell, and I knew it wasn't enough. "I'm sorry, Mason. But why did you come here in the first place? Why did you tell me all of this?"

The gears in his brain were churning as he watched me, his eyes filled with complex sentiments. I could see the moment he decided that any argument he gave wouldn't be good enough.

"I won't prove myself to you forever," he said, "but I'm willing to earn your trust. And the faster the killer is found and locked up, the sooner you might give me a chance. *That's* why I'm here."

Before I could respond, Mason gave me a tentative nod and a ridiculously stiff, but adorable, sort of wave and let himself out through the front gate. I watched him stride away, looking too good in clothes that appeared to have seen better decades. His jeans were worn, molded to him, and his T-shirt was almost threadbare. He'd probably come straight from the garage.

When I turned back to check on Paul, I nearly had a heart attack. I wasn't the only one watching Mason walk away. Bertha had her nose pressed to the window, binoculars pointed directly at me.

"Jeez, Bertha! You need a warning on those things," I called to her. "Do you not believe in privacy?"

"Nope," she said cheerily. "No such thing when you live on the same block as Bertha Broomer."

"Paul, you okay?" I asked, gritting my teeth as I turned away from my Peeping Bertha. "That woman needs to get a life."

So does Mason, Paul said. *Because you just crushed him.*

"I didn't crush him! I'm in the middle of a murder investigation. I have to consider all of my options."

Are you still upset because you didn't consider him right away?

"Maybe," I hedged. "But that's fair. I missed a totally viable suspect."

Or, you just knew him enough to know he hadn't done it.

"That's impossible. I've barely spoken with him."

You've talked every day for the last ... oh, I don't know, month? You have a feel for him.

"Maybe he has a creepy side he hasn't shown yet."

"Or," Paul said, *"maybe you're just afraid to let someone in."*

"You're not Oprah. Leave me alone," I said. "I'm going after Darren. Don't let the slug monster in the house."

I felt a little bad for leaving Paul trembling behind, but his comments had burned. Maybe he had a point. Maybe I wanted to believe Mason was a good man. A man still interested in me, who wanted to take me to dinner.

Still, I couldn't quite believe it — why me? Mason might not be incredibly rich, but he was well enough off and *obviously* handsome. He'd dated a slew of the most beautiful women on the island. It was much easier to believe that he was a psychotic murder schmoozing up to me to throw off suspicion.

The trek to the ferry dock wasn't long. I made the trip in less than twenty minutes at full speed. Despite the bright sun baking my shoulders with warmth, a distant dark cloud loomed on the horizon and I suspected a late afternoon storm. Every watery gene in my body could feel the rain pelting down on the Jersey shore just across the water.

I wondered if this was Skye blowing in another storm just to prove she could. Or, if the trees were right, it might be something more — it might be drawn to the island by a creature that attracted death and decay, thunder and storms, rain and sludge. I sighed. My to-do list had grown exponentially in the last few hours, and not by my choice.

When I reached the ticket kiosk for the ferry, I realized my one crucial error. I hadn't asked anyone for a description of Darren. I'd also not seen a photo of him, and the internet was far too spotty to hope for a window of service that would pull up the image I needed.

Luckily, the pier wasn't crowded. Eternal Springs would be awash with visitors the next few days. If the popularity of this morning's radio segment was anything to go by, tourists would flock to the island to digest the latest gossip and attend the pageant. Ferries would bring far more people than they were taking away until the pageant wrapped. Kenna should pay me for that interview. Her tourism duties would be astronomical and she'd be able to organize to her little heart's content.

After searching the pier from one end to the other and coming up empty, I sighed and hopped in line for the coffee cart. There was no way I had made the trek all the way over here for nothing. I refused to accept anything more than a piping hot latte for my efforts.

The line moved quickly. After ordering, I ran my hands over my arms in a shiver and felt goosebumps prickle my skin. The storm was moving in quickly, a crisp breeze with it.

"Oops, sorry," I said, as I bumped someone. "Didn't see you there."

When I looked up to give the man an apologetic smile, my expression froze. My eyes fixed on the briefcase he held in his hands. It was a clear, plastic sort of thing that was probably supposed to be trendy, though to me it looked silly. However, it was the lettering along the edge that caught my eye.

"Watch where you're going," he scowled. "Bloody hot coffee."

His British accent seeped out as he balanced the Styrofoam cup in his hands and dodged me. I put a hand out, forced the smile, and apologized again.

"Do you work for Elemental Beauty?" I asked, pointing to his bag. "Love the products."

His frown tilted into a more horizontal line. "Yes, they're great."

"Is your name — you're Darren, aren't you?" I tried to keep my voice light, hoping that a bit of goodwill would earn me a few points when I asked the harder questions. "The girls from the Beauty Cottage were raving about you and the products. You're the vendor, right?"

"I am for this contest, yes."

"Latte's ready," the coffee cart guy interrupted. "Here you are, lady."

I reached for the cup and snatched it, turning back before Darren had a chance to move away. "Say, do you mind if I ask you a few questions about the products? I work in radio," I said in a stroke of genius. "And I love to review beauty products."

He looked me over with heavy skepticism. "You know about beauty products?"

"I was working in the yard today," I said, trying to excuse my appearance. "I didn't really get dressed."

"Oh." He seemed to buy my excuse, which didn't say much for my fashion sense. "Wait, are you the woman who interviewed Tarryn?"

"Er ... ." I realized my error as quickly as his face morphed into fury. Tarryn's huge anti-Elemental Beauty rant would *not* be earning me any brownie points.

Darren's eyebrows knit together in a frustration that was probably justified, even if the product line deserved it. "Get out of here! I don't want to say a word to you — you sabotaged our new line!"

"That wasn't me! My name is ... ." I hesitated, thought quickly. "Skye. And I just want to get the facts straight."

"What facts?"

"About the beauty line. I work with a woman who could get a story published to counteract the radio segment. I mean, nobody listens to that show anyway, right? Everybody reads the newspaper. Skye — er, I can get a piece in the Town Croaker if you answer a few questions."

He surveyed me. "I suppose so. That deejay was very unprofessional."

"I don't know about that —."

"She clearly didn't have control over her interview subject."

"Maybe she was taken by surprise," I said, sounding waspish. "But you're right. What do you say — a minute to chat?"

"Fine."

We walked to the nearest bench, but neither of us sat. Eventually I leaned forward against the pier railing and watched the oncoming ferry, calculating I had about five minutes before it docked and began the pre-loading process for passengers.

"I'm not actually here to focus on your beauty products," I said. "I wanted to ask you about the morning you were at the Beauty Cottage. Don't worry, we'll get to the products."

His eyes flickered with unease. He reached for the railing and steadied himself. "What about it?"

"What time did you arrive?"

"Seven thirty."

"I thought most vendors weren't scheduled until later."

"They weren't, but as you might have heard, we are introducing a new line of high-end products. I had scheduled a few consults one on one with the girls and I wanted to get set up early."

"Two and a half hours early?"

"One hour early. The first client was for eight thirty," he said, snippiness creeping into his voice. "It's quite usual for me to arrive an hour early for appointments. I have my case to set up, accessories to spread out. Certain services require hot water, towels, etc. Beauty is not a simple thing, Miss —."

"Skye," I said again, flinching. "Just call me Skye."

"Fine, Skye. Who'd you say you work for again?"

"A radio station. I also have a friend who is a newspaper reporter," I said. "Together, we're sort of covering the beauty pageant."

"And what do the vendors have to do with anything?"

I fastened onto the information I'd gathered from the contestants and did my best to regurgitate it. "Obviously, Elemental Beauty is breaking onto the scene to compete with Loreen — the super high end of beauty products — and we want to cover it. A positive quote from you will go a long way in helping to counteract Tarryn's bad public relations. I'm sure the line is fabulous. Tarryn was probably just upset. After all, she'd just lost a dear friend."

Flattery tended to work for me, and it worked on Darren. He nodded, wary, though attentive.

"As I said, we could get a quick quote from you about the line in the paper. It'll make you and the product line look great."

"Fine. All of that mess about the face cream giving Mary hives — if any of that shows up in your article I will take legal action."

"I understand." I gave him my most sincere expression. "I also hope you understand that I'll need to ask if it was true. Did the cream give Mary issues?"

"Nobody knows!" His face grew red. "She complained to me, but it could have been any of her products. She used a slew of beauty supplies every day."

"And a false claim could ruin your business," I said sympathetically, "especially if Mary was projected to win the pageant."

"Exactly." He smacked his hand so hard against the railing

that a metallic clank rang out and several bystanders turned to stare at us. "Ticks me off, you know? All that hard work goes to waste for one stupid girl."

My eyebrows shot up. "And it'd be much easier to make the problem disappear, wouldn't it?"

"Of course it would. What sort of question is that?" Darren turned to stare at me, still lost in a cloud of rage. "Oh, *crap*. I didn't mean it like that. I didn't mean literally disappear — it came out wrong. You're not here to talk about beauty products at all, are you, Skye?"

"No." I shook my head. "I'm sorry, Darren. My name isn't Skye, and I don't care about face creams."

"You should. You're getting wrinkles, and you can't be much over thirty."

"I'm here to talk about murder."

Darren's face went pale. "I didn't kill Mary."

"Why'd you show up so early two days ago?" I asked him. "That morning was a special occasion, wasn't it? Mary had a meeting marked in her calendar — was it a beauty consultation with you that went horribly wrong?"

That last part was a fib, but he didn't need to know that. I had no access to Mary's phone or calendar, but I needed to push Darren far enough to see if he'd crack.

"Did you go to see Mary the morning she died?" I pressed, as Darren's eyes narrowed. "Maybe you suggested you head out back for natural light while you demonstrated a new foundation. Then, while you were out at the pool, maybe she started complaining about the last sample you gave her. Did she still have hives? That would be pretty tragic for a beauty queen. She must have been fuming."

"No, *no*! That's not how things went."

"Did you find your opportunity and take it? I don't think you meant to strangle her, Darren. I think you just got upset, maybe reached out to give her a push, and things escalated. Is that what happened?"

I gave the railing a light tap with my hand and a soft reverb filtered out through the ocean. Overhead, the sky darkened. Darren's face grew as white as the caps licking the ocean waves. We stood, facing one another, the dark waters slapping against the rocks.

A chill wracked my body and I felt suddenly grateful for the coffee cart just feet away. A family played nearby on a picnic blanket, and a romantic couple leaned against a lamppost in the throes of kissing and giggles. All were within screaming distance, just in case.

"That's not what happened," Darren said finally in a choked voice. "You don't know what you're talking about, Skye — or whatever your name is. You're not a cop, and I don't owe you an explanation."

"I'm Evian Brooks of HEX 66.6, and I was the one who interviewed Tarryn this morning," I said. "I'm covering the murder investigation of Marilyn Johnson, and right now you're not exactly looking innocent. You had motive, access, opportunity. Heck you were at the crime scene at the time of the murder."

"I wasn't, okay? I wasn't there!"

I blinked. "Then where were you?"

"I don't owe you anything."

"No, but I can have the police here in a second. Or, now that my show is actually popular, I could broadcast my theories about your involvement to all of Eternal Springs. That would make things a whole lot worse for you than a short blip about a batch of bad face cream."

"Give me some good exposure for the face cream and I'll talk to you."

"No deals just yet," I said. "Talk first, then I'll discuss."

"I showed up late that day. I didn't want to tell anyone because my boss has been on my case," Darren said, scratching his head as his face flushed. "I didn't arrive until almost eight thirty, even though I was *supposed* to be there at seven thirty. I snuck in, set up shop and I didn't talk to anyone."

"Convenient."

"Sometime closer to nine — I don't know the exact moment — the screams began when the girls saw the body. I packed up and headed out the front door."

"Again, a clear sign of innocence," I said sarcastically. "You didn't want to see what it was about?"

"Lady, I'm already in enough trouble with my boss. I didn't need to add another thing to the mix, I swear. The only person I saw was some guy headed out the back door when I arrived. I didn't get close enough to recognize him because I was in a hurry. Other than that, I stayed in the dining room — alone. I was setting up my station. The other vendors hadn't arrived yet. Most of the girls were still asleep. The door was unlocked when I got there."

I blew out a disgruntled sigh. "Let me get this straight: You not only *accidentally* arrived at the scene of the crime just after the Mary was killed but well before she was found, and you saw a mystery man you can't describe running away."

"I swear it. Ask the girls. I'm sure one of them will have seen me. And they probably saw the other man, too."

"You were running late. Why?"

"Why does anyone run late?" Darren asked. "I'm never on time. I've been written up three times in the last month. You can definitely check that. My boss has been kind enough to document every little one of my screw-ups."

"Oh, I will," I said, though I believed him. Darren had started to perspire and his hands nervously beat against the railing. "What else happened that morning?"

"Nothing! After the scream it was chaos. Someone called

the cops — you must have already been there, actually. You found the body, right? They said it was the radio girl."

"Yes, I did. There was no scream when she died."

"Not before she died, but after." Darren shook his head. "There were nothing but screams in that house as the girls found out what happened."

"You didn't think to come forward with your story and let the police know about some guy running away from the crime scene?"

"Look, Skye — Evian, whatever — listen to how it sounds. My product just gave the dead girl hives and I had a solid motive to want her permanently silenced. I showed up at the scene of the crime and saw a figure running away, but I can't identify if it was a male or female for certain. No." He shook his head. "That's not happening. I look guilty enough."

"Hiding doesn't make you look any less guilty."

"What would you have done? I'm innocent. I didn't see anything. I don't have any helpful information to offer. I'm much better off going home, minding my own business and trying not to lose my job."

"A job that you still have because a girl was found dead."

"Don't you think I know that? Look." Darren pleaded with me. "I didn't tell my boss about Mary because ... I goofed."

I squinted at him. "How do you mean?"

"I need this job — I have serious bills to pay — and Mary is one of my best clients. When she asked for a new sample to review I might have given her something a little special. One that hadn't been FDA approved yet."

I groaned. "Darren. That's a horrible idea."

"I realize that now," he said, his teeth gritted. "I even knew it at the time, but she was my best client. What could I say, no? She asked specifically for it."

"You should have said no! Cripes, Darren! You're lucky all it did was give her hives."

"I know, I know," he said. "And I feel terrible. But I swear to you, I didn't kill her. You have to believe me."

"I'm sorry, Darren, but I think you should stay on the island." I watched as the ferry docked and began unloading its cargo from Jersey. "It doesn't matter if I believe you. The investigation is still open, and the police need all the help they can get."

"Yeah, well, you're not the police." Darren hiked his bag higher onto his arm and plastered a steady look on his face. "I'm sorry Mary's dead — she really was a nice girl. But I didn't do it, and I'm getting off this godforsaken rock. There's still a murderer on the loose."

"Darren —."

He glanced over his shoulder as a crack of thunder boomed overhead. As he met my eyes, he smiled. The smile sent a jolt through me, accented by a streak of lightning that looked close enough to zap the waters beneath the ferry.

I stayed in place, unable to leave Eternal Springs thanks to my past. The ferry loaded up as I helplessly watched, and in a few moments the captain signaled a goodbye toot of the horn and chugged away from the pier, carrying a potential murderer back to Jersey.

Sixteen

Just my luck — the rain started to fall the second I began the trek home.

Worse, I'd been so distracted by Darren that I hadn't had the chance to finish my latte, which left me with the choice to jog home and spill it on the way or stroll slowly, finish the latte, and get drenched.

I opted for a mix of the two, walking at a quick pace until the latte was gone. Then, fueled by the quick jolt of energy, I dumped the empty cup in a garbage can and picked up the pace in a jog toward home. Heaving for breath, I slowed to a walk when I reached my street.

As my house came into view I felt my energy beginning to wane, as if the very core of me was exhausted. My feet dragged, my eyes prickled with tears and my very motivation to solve this case began to feel heavy and pointless. Not only was I soaked, but I'd made several enemies with my snooping. Despite all my work, I was no closer to finding the murderer.

Any number of people could have killed Mary. The opportunities were there: Mason walking past the scene of the crime, all the girls living in the cottage where the victim was killed, and Darren, whose story was just a little too convenient. Add in the potential for a mystery man or woman and the options were almost endless.

I sighed, glancing up to find Bertha's binoculars pressed to her window. The woman never quit. If only she'd bought property next to the Beauty Cottage instead of my house, maybe she would've seen the murder take place and solved this thing for everyone.

Instead, she stared at me, mysterious invisible slugs and the empty road. With a start, I latched onto that last piece — *the empty road*. Could she have seen a man running away from the Beauty Cottage? If Darren had been right, maybe Bertha had caught a glimpse of the figure if he'd turned up the road and come our way.

I made a sharp turn and strode up to the window. I rapped my knuckles against the glass, barely hiding a grin as Bertha leapt, startled, from her seat. If only she hadn't been staring through my front windows, maybe she would've noticed what was right before her.

"What do you think you're doing?" Bertha snapped as she hauled the window open. "Privacy goes one way, young lady. I'm old. I've earned the right to peep."

"I'm actually here to discuss the pros of your peeping," I said. "The other day — the morning of Mary's murder — did you see anyone leaving the Beauty Cottage between eight and eight thirty?"

She frowned. "Well, obviously I saw you run into Mason that day. Speaking of that, are you ever going to accept his offer of a date? It's quite clear he's into you."

Fuming, I shrugged. "I don't know. Anyone else?"

"Well, Edwin, but I figured he was organizing the girls for whatever press junket they were on for the day."

"Wait a second," I said. "You saw Edwin leaving the Beauty Cottage?"

"Yes. He's the little coordinator man, correct? Hold on a second." Bertha disappeared from the window and returned a second later holding a pageant program. "I nabbed myself one of these so I could see who I was spying on." She tapped her forehead and it gave a hollow sort of thunk. "I'm a real thinker."

"You have years of experience," I said. "You're a snooper extraordinaire."

"That I am." She happily flipped through the pages of the program, landing on the photo of Edwin. "Yep! I knew I was right. Edwin is this one."

"Was he in a hurry?"

"He's always in a hurry when he comes and goes. The man doesn't have a slow button. Or at least, it looked that way from here."

"Does he come and go a lot?"

"Just twice. That morning and once before. He didn't stay long either time."

"Thanks, Bertha," I said, and turned away. "Continue peeping."

"Wait a second, you didn't tell me why! Did I help crack a case?"

"We'll see," I said. "I don't know yet."

Bertha slammed her window shut, plopped down on her seat, and fished a pair of binoculars from her lap. She propped them against the window and resumed her favorite afternoon activity.

I slipped and slid up the front of my walkway, which was now slick with mud. When I made it inside I promptly peeled off my outer layers and left them on the porch. I continued to the bathroom, where I peeled off my inner layers and climbed under the blissfully hot stream of water, soaking in the lavender-scented soap and honeysuckle shampoo. I was halfway through the steamiest shower I could muster when yet another voice invaded my home.

"This is the coven," Margaret's voice rang through the room. "Get dressed, Evian. We must talk."

I reached for my towel and tried to calm my racing heart. "How about some warning?" I clutched the fabric to my chest and pulled the shower curtain back just enough to reveal my face. "This is my private space!"

"Yes, well, you're the water witch. We speak to you via water," Margaret, the second in command, said, sounding bored. "Hurry. The rest of us will be here shortly."

Margaret's reflection appeared in the steamy fog of my mirror. I had the urge to swipe it off, but I didn't. The coven was already annoyed with me as a general principle, and I didn't want to give the members any reasons to use their curses.

I ducked out of sight and slipped into a bathrobe, shrugging everything into position so that the council wouldn't have to see body parts that would leave them with nightmares. I wished we could find a new artifact to communicate through besides the bathroom mirror, but they were insistent.

"Is everyone there?" I asked Margaret. "Who all is joining today?"

"Enough of us," she said vaguely. "Now, Evian Brooks, it has been brought to our attention that there is portal activity in Eternal Springs."

"That has not been confirmed." I crossed my arms. "Yes, there's something that seems to be slinking around here and killing my plants, but for all I know it could just be some dirt-transmitted virus or something."

"Why do I doubt that's the case?"

"I don't know what is wrong, so if you feel like enlightening me, go right ahead," I said, trying to keep the annoyance from my voice. "All I'm saying is that something is killing my lawn. I have no clue if it's from the portal."

"Your familiar seems to think otherwise."

"Paul snitched on me?!" I glanced around for the toad, but he had probably heard the coven's call and retired somewhere out of reach. "I will kill him!"

"Familiars are bound to transmit certain information to the coven, Evian, you know this. It's not only to protect them but to protect you, as well as the rest of our kind."

"Well, I'm not feeling very understanding right now. All Paul is basing his hunch on is a possible glimpse of an invisible-to-humans creature."

Even Margaret looked unconvinced at this. "That's it?"

"That's it. Nobody else saw this thing. My neighbor was looking through the window with her binoculars as she always does and didn't see a thing. Or, at least I assume she didn't. She would have said something if she saw a monster in my yard."

"How is Bertha?" Margaret leaned forward, a slim smile on her face. "I haven't talked to her in too long."

"How do you know Bertha?"

"When we conduct our routine checks of the island I'll often stop in and say hello to her," she said. "After all, Bertha is the best source of gossip in Eternal Springs."

"No, she's not. She doesn't leave the house to get fresh gossip."

"She pays attention to what you do every minute of the day." Margaret could barely hide her smile. "And you and the other three are the only ones we care to check up on, anyway."

"You use Bertha to spy on me?"

"You make it sound so formal and invasive."

"Well, it is," I said. "I wish you'd let me have some privacy."

"I wish the four of you had paid attention thirteen years ago," Margaret shot back. "Because you didn't, it's hard to assume that any of you are paying attention these days. Especially when I'm getting reports of portal activity that you are harshly denying."

"I'm not harshly denying anything, I simply don't know the facts. There might be portal activity, and if there is, I'll give you a call and let you know."

"Finally, we have reached an understanding. Can we trust that you'll look into this mess and get to the ... ." She paused for a laugh, "*root* of the problem?"

I squinted at Margaret. "Hilarious. But it's not your plants that are dying."

"No, it's not, but it sounds as if the rest of Eternal Springs will be experiencing sludge in their yards if you don't get rid of the issue. Paul explained that Bertha was already complaining about her raspberries being affected."

"Why *me*?" I asked. "Why would a portal monster come and attack me, and only me? There's plenty of other land and plants between me and the portal. Why not hit up Cackleberries?"

"How do you water your plants?"

"Excuse me?"

"How do you water your plants?" Margaret asked again. "It's a serious question."

"Well ... ." I shifted uncomfortably from one foot to the next. "You know, a little bit of this, a little bit of that."

"Magic."

"I guess," I said, hedging defensively. "But I'm a water witch! It's in my nature. How else do you expect me to stretch my magical muscles?"

"I trust you're doing it when Bertha's not watching?"

"*Sprinkle water under a new full moon; then watch your garden grow and bloom*," I said. "It's a little booster spell my mother taught me. If I use the spell once a month under the full moon, my garden flourishes. Except this time around, of course."

Margaret nodded. "I'd imagine that the monster is attracted to the magical activity in your yard. When you infuse water with magic, it's tainted. Enchanted, if you will. You can't simply get rid of the magical traces just because the water seeps into the ground."

"So you think that this monster pops up from the portal, travels to my house," I said, "and comes to feed on the water I use for my plants?"

"I wouldn't be surprised if the creature isn't doing this maliciously," Margaret said. "It could be he's doing what feels right to him, and it just so happens the monster destroys everything he touches."

"How?"

She shrugged. "Any number of ways. He might feed on life and growth while leaving behind destruction. The more light he takes in, the more darkness he leaves behind."

I sighed. "Sounds like a big task to get rid of him."

"You're up for the job," Margaret said with a chipper grin. "And if you're not, you can die trying."

"You don't mean that, do you?"

"I think we're just about done here." She pointedly ignored my question. "Goodbye, Evian —."

"Wait! No help? You're not sending anyone here?"

"It's not our mess to clean up. None of us wanted the portal opened. If you need help, ask those friends of yours. There are plenty of you in Eternal Springs to take care of this mess. And besides, we've got some political issues in the coven that need urgent addressing. I'm sorry, we don't have personnel to spare."

"Fine," I snapped. "We'll take care of it, no thanks to you.

But I have one favor to ask — and you don't have to come to Eternal Springs to take care of it."

"What sort of favor?"

"There's been a murder."

"Marilyn Johnson from Jersey, yes," Margaret muttered a sympathetic cluck. "How unfortunate. She seemed like a nice girl. And I was excited about seeing her win the pageant."

"Yes, so you heard about her demise."

"We listen to your radio show," one of them said. "Your channel comes in very clear over here, and we don't get any of that calypso crap that seems to be on repeat on the island. We actually hear the songs you and Leonard are trying to play."

"How is that possible?!"

"Magic isn't as concentrated outside of Eternal Springs," she said patiently. "It doesn't mess with the transmission waves or whatever they're called. Signals. All that technical junk. The coven has even considered handing out cell phones to its members. Isn't that fun?"

"Delightful," I said. "Can we get back to my problem now?"

Margaret heaved a heavy sigh. "You have so many problems, Evian. What is it now?"

"Well, you probably heard the radio segment with Tarryn the other day ... ."

"Yes."

"Then you heard her claims against Elemental Beauty products."

"I believe the word 'hives' was used," Margaret said. "I'm glad for the warning because I was just about to purchase some hand lotion for the coven's main offices. Can you imagine what a disaster that would have been if it caused hives all around? How awful."

"Quite the catastrophe. Anyway," I said. "I have

continued trying to track down Mary's killer, and I have a good reason to believe that Darren Whiting is a suspect to keep an eye on. He's the vendor for the Elemental Beauty line at this pageant, and he had motive and opportunity to kill Mary. He was at the Beauty Cottage during the time of her death — or close to it. He doesn't have a good alibi. If he didn't silence Mary, he might have lost his job."

"I don't see how we can help," Margaret said. "Our advice is to steer clear from human interference as much as possible, especially on the mainland. It's not our job to press and prod and poke and pry. We've tried that route before, and trust me, it's not the best way to do things."

"I don't need you to *seriously* interfere, I just need you to tip your hand a tiny bit. To detain Darren for me."

"Detain him how? Where?"

"I'm going to the police station to give them the information I have," I said. "But Darren is already on the ferry to Jersey. It might be too late if he reaches land before the cops get after him. If he disappears, we may never find him."

"It's not our job to interfere," Margaret said again. "Mixing magic and humans is never a good idea."

"This is an isolated incident. Just give me twenty-four hours. Hole him up somewhere, distract him for a bit. Please, I'm begging you. Do it for Mary."

"The pageant won't be the same without Mary." Margaret frowned. "Whoever *did* murder her deserves to be punished."

"Yes! That's why I'm looking so hard into this case. Please, I'm begging you. Twenty-four hours is all I'm asking, and then you can let him go if I don't have enough evidence. He'll be none the wiser if you wipe his memory."

"Give me a second." Margaret turned away from the mirror and spoke in flurried whispers among her peers. There was a lot of nodding and obscure language and blurred faces. Not enough to make out a word of what was said. Finally,

Margaret returned and offered me a smile. "As it turns out, Marilyn Johnson had a lot of fans in coven headquarters, what with her being from Jersey and all. We have agreed to help you."

"Oh, thank you," I said. "Thank you so much."

"For the next twenty-four hours," she said with a thin smile, "Darren Whiting will be under a love spell. We'll have a pillow sent to his room, and he'll be convinced it's 'the one.' He won't be going anywhere."

"Thank you, thank you," I said. "You won't regret this."

"After that, *poof!*" Margaret warned. "He'll snap out of it like Cinderella's pumpkin."

"Understood," I said. "Thank you again for —."

Margaret disappeared with a small crackle of magic, leaving me talking only to my reflection in the mirror.

"Thanks for your help," I muttered. "Nice chatting with you all."

I quickly got dressed, my mind clicking through the to-do list I needed to accomplish before the love spell on Darren broke. I needed to go to the police — I owed them the information I'd uncovered so far. Maybe they could follow Darren to Jersey. Then I needed to prepare for the opening night of the beauty pageant at Coconuts. The pageant's first official day was tomorrow, and Kenna had scheduled a huge kickoff karaoke event for tonight. Checking the clock, I realized it was only a few hours away. *Everyone* would be there, so it would be the perfect place to keep an eye out for interactions between my suspects. It'd be more interesting to see if anyone was conveniently missing from the festivities.

But before I did either of those things, I needed to have an adult conversation with Paul.

"You snitch!" I accused, finding him tucked under the covers on the porch. "I can't believe you ratted me out to the coven."

I didn't have a choice, Paul whined. *They threatened to take away my ability to talk to you if I didn't tell them everything I knew about the portal activity.*

"But we don't know for sure what you saw was portal activity."

You're in denial, I know what I saw, woman. I saw a portal monster.

"Fine," I said. "Then you can help me track it down. Get your raincoat."

You know I hate getting wet. And mud? Paul shuddered. *I think I'll stay in bed.*

"Get dressed," I ordered. "I'm going to the police station first, and when I come back you and I are going on a monster hunt."

Seventeen

It was an odd sort of day.

I'd chased down a murder suspect, gotten reamed on the radio and sprinted a mile through a raging storm — and this evening's agenda wasn't looking any better. If I'd calculated correctly, I'd be headed to the police station first, then off to hunt a swamp monster and choose a crowd-pleasing karaoke jam.

Dressing for such an occasion was nearly impossible.

I finally settled on jeans, flats and one of my favorite T-shirts that said *Resting Witch Face* on it. I'd bought it because Kenna had one, and it always annoyed her to match. Then I'd shrugged on a dandelion yellow raincoat, because really, what other color looked good in that weird plastic material?

That is how I found myself standing outside the police station decked out in a raincoat on a perfectly sunny afternoon. Apparently the storm had blown briefly over the island. It'd stayed just long enough to make me look like a complete moron. By the time I reached the station it was a gorgeous, perfect-golfing-weather afternoon.

I shrugged out of the coat before heading inside. I asked

at the front desk to speak to whichever cop was available. It wasn't as if Eternal Springs was large enough to have a large force.

I was eventually shown to an interview room and given a seat, offered coffee — which I accepted — and was told to wait. As I waited, I reviewed what I wanted to tell the cops. Everything from my interviews with the girls to my chase of Darren to the mystery man (most likely Edwin) at the crime scene.

"Good afternoon, Evian," Burt, one of the handful of rent-a-cops on the island grinned as he entered the room. "What brings you here today?"

"I have some information I want to share with you regarding Marilyn Johnson's murder."

"I heard the show earlier." Burt winced. "*Ouch*, am I right?"

"Yeah, thanks. It feels really good that you're reminding me about it right now."

"That Tarryn is a firecracker, all right." He gave a low whistle and completely missed my sarcasm. "Almost makes a guy wonder if she was capable of offing her friend. She's projected to win the whole pageant, I hear, now that Mary's gone."

"So they're saying," I said. "Well, look. I've been asking around some in my spare time —."

"Interfering with the investigation, I hear." Burt gave a chuckle. "You know that's our job, Miss Brooks, don't you?"

"I just felt bad. After all, I was the one who discovered the body."

Burt's face went somber. "I understand. Do you want to amend your initial statement from the crime scene?"

"Sort of," I said, "though it's not only my statement. Like I said, I've talked to a few people who knew Mary and, well … ." I sighed. "You might want a notebook for this."

"Better yet, how about we do this?" Burt set a small digital recorder on the table before me. He flicked it to *on* and the red light blinked. Quickly, he recorded the date, time and our names, and then gave me a nod. "Go ahead, Miss Brooks."

I laid everything out for him in one long — hopefully organized — stream of consciousness. I started with my suspicions of the medical examiner, which made Burt frown. Nobody liked to think one of "our own" had participated in a murder. Abigail might not be an ME by choice, but she was supposed to *help* the police, not cover up evidence.

I followed up my thoughts on Abigail with her link to Mason, and Mason's link to Mary. Then I filled Burt in on my chats with Edwin, Carl and the beauty pageant contestants, including the newest tidbit that Bertha might have seen Edwin at the cottage around murder o'clock. I concluded with my thoughts on Tarryn and my breakthrough with Darren. I obviously left out the part about calling the coven and requesting love spells.

Burt quickly thanked me as I finished and then switched off the recorder. "Look, Evian, it'd be nice and all if the Jersey cops worked with us, but things ain't that easy. I'm not sure that we can do anything to hold up Darren."

"This is a murder investigation and there's a very real chance that he's our guy. He has a temper," I said, thinking of the metallic clang that had lingered in the air after he lost his cool this afternoon. "I saw it."

"I'm not saying this guy did or didn't hurt Mary, but we don't have any real evidence."

"He was there! He admits to being at the house around the time of the murder." My fingers clenched the edge of the table. "Did anyone question him?"

Burt shifted uncomfortably in his seat. "Well, you see, we were busy that morning. There're only two of us."

"A woman was *murdered*! I understand there aren't many

crimes on the island, which is all the more reason we can't let this one go," I said. "We have to hunt Darren down and question him at the very least."

"Miss Brooks, I would like you to know on behalf of the department that we appreciate your help, but there are certain limitations to what we can do with a force of two people. Unfortunately, Buddy's golf cart can't drive across the ocean, or I'd send him."

"It doesn't feel like you're even trying."

"Of course we're trying." His eyes narrowed, darkened. "It seems to me, Evian, that you're forgetting you don't have a badge. None of us have complained about you playing Nancy Drew and asking around, but we could really get on your case about it if you push things too far. I'm going to say this one more time: Thanks for your help, Miss Brooks. We'll take it from here."

I sensed my time at the station had come to a close. Nothing more would be accomplished by sticking around and forcing my hand. However, if I left on decent terms there was a good chance I could continue asking questions around the island. If I uncovered more evidence on Darren in the next twenty-four hours I'd contact the Jersey police myself.

"Thanks, Burt," I said. "I appreciate you listening."

"There we go. I knew you'd see things my way."

It was all I could do to shake his pudgy hand and follow him out front. Burt whistled as he walked me out, and if I wasn't mistaken he slammed the glass doors just a little too hard as I walked down the front steps.

I sighed on the sidewalk, thinking that if someone would just give me a badge maybe I could actually accomplish something around here. Buddy gave himself awards all the time, why couldn't I turn myself into a cop?

Glancing down, I realized I was still holding the cup of coffee that someone had delivered to me in the interview room. I chugged it, then dumped the cup in a garbage can while debating where to go next.

"Howdy there, Evian," a voice boomed behind me. "What are you doing here at the station? Out looking for trouble?"

The telltale sounds of a golf cart combined with the clacking of knitting needles signaled the mayor's arrival. "Hi, Buddy, Mitzi," I said, forcing a smile and greeting the couple. "No trouble here — just checking in on things. What brings you around?"

The mayor looked beyond me into the building with a longing expression. It would appear Buddy wanted to go inside the station, but after careful consideration had decided the idea of leaving his golf cart throne was much too exhausting. "I thought I'd check in and see how the investigation on Mary's murder was going. Have you heard anything?"

"Not all that much," I said. "I was just talking to Burt about it, so I'm sure he can give you the lowdown."

Buddy gave a hefty sigh. "Never mind. I guess I'll catch up with Burt tonight at the event. Did you hear I won the best-dressed last week at karaoke?"

"I did not hear that, Buddy. Congrats. Who gave you the award?"

His cheeks turned red because obviously it was another self-given accolade. "Will we be seeing you at Coconuts, Evian?"

"Of course. Wouldn't miss it — everyone will be there!" I said with false cheeriness. "What about you, Mitzi?"

"Yep," she drawled. "Got my song picked out and everything. Didn't you listen to the show last week? I talked about it for half an hour!"

"Oh, er, right. I was busy. Sorry." I winced. I always told Mitzi she did a wonderful job, and then promised myself I'd listen in at *some* point. That point hadn't yet arrived.

"What are you singing?" she sniffed. "I didn't hear you talk about it on your show. That's right, I listen to *you*."

"Oh, I don't sing," I said. "That's Kenna's thing."

"She does have a good set of pipes on her," Buddy said with admiration. His wife showed her displeasure at the compliment by nearly slicing her fingers off with the *click, click, click* of her knitting. He coughed. "Forget it. I suppose we'll be seeing you then, Evian."

The mayor's foot must have slipped and hit the gas pedal because the cart lurched forward and Mitzi's needles nearly poked the mayor's eye out. I briefly wondered if it had *actually* been an accident or if she'd aimed there after Buddy's crack about Kenna.

"Well, we're off!" The mayor chortled over his shoulder. "See you tonight, Evian! Don't forget your tunes!"

My walk back to the house was not as sunny as the walk to the police station. The bright rays of sunlight had dissipated behind a thick covering of clouds, and if I wasn't mistaken, another storm was brewing in the distance. Highly unusual weather for this time of year, which made me think it wasn't all natural. Both Paul, the coven and the snarky trees seemed to agree.

My depression reached a new low as I realized Kenna would be shoving me up on stage in just a few hours. There was no such thing as *refusing* to sing karaoke at Coconuts when one was pretend friends with Kenna. Being pretend friends helped keep our witchiness under wraps, because most locals thought we were four weirdos who hung out together. It worked for us.

But I couldn't ditch tonight's event. *Everyone* would be there. It was my one chance to watch everyone close to Mary interact under one roof. The chance the murderer would be in attendance was almost one-hundred percent.

I thought through the list and marked down mental

RSVPs: Abigail would be there, certainly. She never missed the chance to flaunt her newly inflated fake chest. The beauty contestants would also be in attendance vying for media attention — the pageant started tomorrow, after all. The coaches and coordinators would be chaperoning the girls, and the townsfolk would flock to a bar that promised beautiful women. Yes, that included Mason.

By the time I reached home, the raincoat turned out to be an effective choice. I shrugged it back on as droplets started to fall on my shoulders. Pulling the door open, I yelled for Paul. He ignored me the first few times until I threatened to make him sleep outside.

At my empty threat, he hopped onto the porch and sat looking fat and adorable. I didn't normally describe a toad — even a familiar to whom I was obligated to feel fondness now and again — as adorable, but in this case, it was accurate.

Paul had dressed in a matching bright yellow raincoat and tiny little hat. He even wore little booties that made his leaps completely ineffective. He and I matched perfectly. Kenna would be horrified.

Keep your mouth shut, Paul directed, *and pick me up already.*

I smothered a laugh as I reached for him. With a gentle scoop, I plopped him on my shoulder. "Come on, Paul," I said. "We're going on a monster hunt."

Eighteen

"Which way?" I asked. "Did you see which way the monster went?"

No.

"How about a guess?"

Nope.

"Gee, you're helpful," I snarled, standing at my front gate. Bertha stared me down through her binoculars. "Give me your best estimate. You saw more than I did."

I don't know, and I don't want to be here. I'm just an innocent victim.

"Well, you're stuck with me, pal, so we're in this together." I scanned my yard in the hope it would give me a push in the right direction. "I hadn't realized how bad things have gotten out here."

You've been busy, and your yard's not the only thing that's been neglected.

While he pouted I raised a hand and gave him a little pat on the head. He wriggled closer to my fingers and gave a low croak of satisfaction. With my familiar slightly appeased, I took a longer moment to study the destruction before my house.

The yard had turned into a giant mud bath. Even the pale sidewalks were streaked with dirt and mud, as if a child had haphazardly finger-painted along them with soil. The garden beds overflowed with fossils of flowers and remnants of former beauty. It was no more than a vacant cemetery in a sea of muck.

I wrinkled my nose, aware that Bertha probably saw every line on my skin through her binoculars. Even as I stood there, I heard her window fly up.

"Are you getting Zola to look at your lawn?" Bertha called out. "I've never seen such a disaster in all my life."

"Thanks, Bertha."

"You'd better watch or it's gonna eat my raspberries alive, and I'm gonna have to ask you for compensation. Those bad boys took a lot of love and hard work to grow."

Bertha meant she'd hired the local garden boys to plunk some bushes along our shared fence. From there, she'd let the rain take care of the watering. The love and hard work must be referring to her spying habits.

"It's even creeping up that way!" Bertha swung her binoculars around to the back of my house where a narrow dark path led toward the woods. It hadn't been there before, of that I was certain. "I imagine the town council isn't gonna be too excited to see this. If whatever bug got into your dirt wipes out the whole forest they'll hunt you down."

"Not if the coven or a giant destructive slug eats me first," I said, gritting my teeth. Then, I called to her. "Thanks, Bertha. I'm going to go investigate now."

"Your investigating isn't doing much good now, is it?" Bertha said. "You haven't found that murderer you've been looking for yet. Have you forgotten about that?"

"No, Bertha, I haven't. Thanks for pointing out all of my

shortcomings." I followed the sidewalk around the house and picked up the sludge trail in my backyard. "I'll see you in a bit."

"Good luck out there. Make sure to call Zola — she knows how to take care of plants and flowers. These raspberries are from Cackleberries, you know."

Of course I knew, but I bit back the snarky comment. I'd had to help the garden boy from Zola's shop put the raspberries in place while Bertha had watched. And Bertha didn't even let me have any berries when they were ripe. She wanted to charge me five bucks for a small box of them. And they called *me* the witch.

Look at that ugly line, Paul said. *I'll bet he went that way.*

Indeed, there was an odd, squiggly sort of path through the back of my yard that continued out into the field beyond. Luckily, no houses stood between mine and the portal. It was mostly unoccupied wilderness, open fields and walking trails that extended from the main hotel and spa.

Eternal Springs boasted miles of trails and parks and outdoor fitness activities for those folks arriving in hopes of leaving ten pounds lighter. In reality, the walking trails were mostly used by the locals whose dogs pulled their owners out for fresh air and a stretch of the legs. Eternal Springs was more of a sprucing sort of place, where people wanted to sit around and eat bon bons and lose weight instead of actually *work* for it — Paul included.

Paul and I followed the path in the ground through a series of loops and spirals and wiggly lines. I wondered if the monster had no sense of direction and had been hopelessly lost for his entire journey. Either that or he was drunk on dirt, because the path made no sense whatsoever. Maybe he'd gotten into the Babbling Brook — a river that could have gotten him drunk.

Looks like a slug, doesn't it? Like the big old monster was slithering around here.

"How did nobody see him?" I murmured to Paul. "There's always someone walking their dog. Or, if he's as big as you say, someone should've seen him from the road."

I think he's got some sort of invisibility that prevents the humans from laying eyes on him. A safety measure.

I frowned. "Portal magic is weird. Why'd he have to attack me, anyway? It would make more sense to go after Zola. She's got a whole shop full of plants."

Oh, there he went — look. I think that's the end of the road.

"Where is he going?" I mused, as we followed the trajectory downhill. Suddenly the imprinted rut on the ground turned from squiggly to straight, as if the monster had found what he was looking for and made a beeline toward it. Another minute of following the path and it was easy to see where he'd been headed.

"Water," I said, as Paul croaked in agreement. "It was headed toward the water."

Good riddance. It needed a bath.

The sound of gurgling water drew us toward the riverbank. A rocky swath of land separated the grass from a pale white line of sand, beyond which a stream frothed its way over and under fallen logs, jagged boulders and the underwater forest of seaweed and plants.

This stream goes right by the portal. Water is probably the easiest way for him to travel.

"Maybe," I said, "but that means he could be anywhere. Ugh, we have to find him! If we don't he'll start drawing attention to himself and people will be asking questions I can't answer."

It'll be worse than that. They'll be looking to blame you. The destruction is worst in your yard.

"You really know how to make me feel better."

I'm just being honest. Everyone thinks you're weird enough as is.

I bit my lip and decided to pick my way through the rocky pass. The soles of my shoes were so thin I could feel every ridge and bump as Paul directed me over the path of least resistance. When I finally reached the silky sand spreading along the river, my feet were quite relieved.

Hold up. That's one lazy monster.

"What are you talking about?"

Shush! Look.

There, just around the bend in the river, I caught a glimpse of a shiny, slick skin that could only belong to a paranormal creature. It sparkled in the sunlight, an odd, purplish sheen beneath the layer of translucence.

You can see that thing, right? I'm not going crazy?

"Oh, you're crazy, but I see it."

You're hilarious. So, what are you going to do about him?

"I-I don't know." I inched forward, cautiously, so as to not draw attention to myself. "This isn't working. That pile of rocks is obstructing my view. I need to get closer."

I think it's better to keep your distance from monsters, Paul said. *Just my opinion.*

"Someone has to put him back into the realm where he belongs," I pointed out. "Looks like it's going to be me because I don't have another option. The other three girls don't believe me, and the coven has made it clear where it stands."

Ask for help! The only reason they didn't believe you is because they don't trust me. Granted, I do tend to embellish my stories.

"Yes, you do," I agreed. "Which is why I need a clear view to see this monster for myself."

I'm out of here. Paul hopped off my shoulder and landed on a slippery rock. Because he was wearing little booties, he didn't get the traction he normally got from his amphibian feet — which resulted in a long slide and a plop onto the sandy shore. *Go on, then — I'll wait right here for you.*

"Remind me to file a petition with the coven for a new sidekick," I muttered, "someone who'll actually watch my back."

Oh, I'll watch your back all right. I'll watch it carefully as you walk into danger, but that's all you can expect from me. I don't plan to follow you to your slimy death.

Ignoring my familiar, I crept quietly over the sandy path until I reached the boulders, stones and rocks that sat in a loosely interwoven pile and blocked my view of the creature. I feared that one wrong touch of a stone would send the whole thing cascading to the ground, so I very carefully rested my fingertips on the sturdiest of rocks.

With extreme caution, I tiptoed to a safe little niche with a perfect window between stones. Two boulders teetered precariously against one another, and through them I caught the first glimpse of the monster that'd come to terrorize Eternal Springs.

"Wow," I gasped, and Paul agreed from a distance with a low croak. "He's huge!"

I told you, Paul said in our unique little language. *But nobody believed me.*

I apologized and promised him a double margarita bath with an extra twist of lemon when we got home. He seemed satisfied with the offer, and I turned my attention back to the river.

Sure enough, the slug was there, bathing in the water, giant and unmistakable. A weird mixture between worm, caterpillar and Barney-the-purple-dinosaur, the creature was long and fat and gooey. As I watched, the thing bent its head and snapped up an entire bush of fresh flowers dangling above the riverbed.

The slug shuddered with happiness. The outer layer of the

animal began to turn black, as if sweating mud. That sludge, I realized, was what had killed my yard, along with the grass and shrubbery that'd been in its way along the path from my house to the river. It apparently feasted on fresh plants, then immediately let loose a toxic barrage of sludge. *Gross!*

If I had to guess, I'd say the slug preferred spending time in water instead of chugging about on land. I sensed he was drawn to it, much like me. I was willing to bet he, too, felt the lunar pull of the changing tides, the gasp of relief as a storm opened its clouds and rained down. I even enjoyed the pleasant sensation of climbing into a shower at the end of the day, just to be reunited with my favored element.

If it was true what Paul said about the slug being invisible to the human eye — which seemed entirely likely because I was certain Bertha would have complained about a fat purple monster — then I had to imagine the sparkling sheen around its outer layer was some sort of magical defense to keep the animal hidden from view. In a way, it was quite impressive, as invisibility was no easy task.

The biggest issue facing me at the moment was *size*. I had to get this big guy back to the portal and send him home — the sooner the better. In a fight, however, I couldn't win — the monster was simply too big. Even if I knocked him unconscious with a spell, I couldn't move him.

That left me with one option: I'd have to corral him to the portal somehow. Herd him, like sheep — except instead of cute fluffy sheep, I'd be herding a giant gross slug. *Just my luck.*

Paul must have heard my mumblings because he approved of the idea with a croak. As I turned to ask him for any ideas, my hand slipped from its perch on the rock and my worst nightmare was realized. One of the stones that'd been guarding my hiding spot let loose and went tumbling to the ground.

Unfortunately, it was a pivotal stone in the tower. The tense silence lasted for an extended second before the clattering began. The next second, everything went haywire.

The pile crumbled and groaned, then clattered to the ground with a grating cacophony of rock-on-rock. The slide started from the midsection and loosed all the top rocks first. I barely managed to jump out of the way as a stone the size of my head landed where my foot had been just moments before.

Smooth, Evian. Now, run!

I dodged back to Paul, scooped him up, and didn't look behind me until I'd pulled us into the trees beyond the riverbank. Only then did I pause for breath. Chancing a glance backward, I found an empty stream where the monster had been moments before.

I needn't have worried; judging by the slug's lack of pursuit, it was more afraid of me than I was of it. The creature had simply vanished.

"Where'd he go?" I asked Paul. "Did you see?"

He disappeared.

"He didn't disappear! He's got to be around here somewhere. Did he hide? How could he possibly hide? He's the size of a tree." I peered across the rocks, the sand, to the water moving into a calm stillness. "He must have taken off."

All I know is that I'm not investigating. This is outside the realm of toadly duties.

"I need to get him closer to the portal."

He seems like a doofus. He's afraid of you, which is just ridiculous.

"I can be scary."

Sure, before you fix your hair in the morning, you can be quite frightening.

I glared at Paul. "What's your theory then? Why's he destroying all growing things?"

I think he stumbled out of the portal and needs a way back. He can't help what he is. The destruction seems to come from the slime on his skin — not something he's doing maliciously.

"I'm not taking any chances," I said. "Maybe if I can get the girls to help ... ."

Yeah, right. You saw the monster first — you know the rules.

"True." I thought for a moment. "Well, we do know what he likes. He likes fresh flowers, life, plants."

But not all plants, or else he would've never bothered to stumble up into your yard and attack it. He seems a lazy monster to me, so there must be something special about your grass.

"Touché." I considered the magical tinge that I used to water my plants. Margaret might be right, though I hated to admit it. "Wait — I've got it, Paul!"

Feel like sharing?

"I'm going to ask Zola for all of the extra plants she has — you know, half-dead daffodils, daisies, whatever. I'll plop them down in a path to the portal, and then I'll use my spell to water them. The full moon is tonight — it will be perfect!"

No wonder today's been so crazy. Witches are always weird around full moons. I should probably stay home in bed. What do I know? You might go dancing naked around a bonfire.

I wrinkled my nose at the thought. "I can't even do karaoke fully clothed. No dancing naked for me."

I suppose your plan is worth a shot. He's gone into hiding for now, anyway.

"Let's swing by Cackleberries on the walk back," I said. "I will seriously owe Zola if she agrees to help."

Before I could take a step toward the witchy garden shop, pattering footsteps sounded on a path through the woods a little too close for comfort. The huff of heavy breathing followed next.

"Hello," a voice said behind me. "Is that you, Evian? What brings you all the way out here ... alone?"

Nineteen

"What are you doing out this way?" Susanne, one of the pageant contestants, slowed from a jog and walked the rest of the distance between us. "I never see anyone out this way."

"Hi," I said, my heart pounding as relief flooded through me. I don't know who I'd expected — the murderer out for a jog? — but the heavy breathing had sent goosebumps across my skin. I gathered my senses and glanced behind me to make sure the huge, supernatural monster wasn't visible. "Just out for a walk. What about you?"

She gestured to herself, implying my question was silly. Then again, she was wearing spandex shorts and a complex-looking sports bra that strapped her chest in such a way that made me think she was prepared to launch into space.

"Exercise," she said, then laughed. "*Obviously.*"

Something you're unfamiliar with, Paul croaked in my ear.

"Right," I echoed through gritted teeth. Talking to my toad was generally frowned upon in public, but if I were in an arguing mood I'd let Paul know that chasing paranormal creatures around Eternal Springs and being dragged to karaoke burned enough calories to call both activities *exercise*. "Do you do that a lot?"

"What, exercise?" Susanne gave another tinkling laugh. "Yes, I try to get in at least one run a day, sometimes two."

"*Two* runs in *one* day?" My jaw fell open. "Every day?"

"That's the goal!" She patted her uber-flat stomach. "Have to keep the weight off somehow. They don't call them beauty contests for nothing."

"I thought it was a pageant."

Susanne bit her lip, her eyebrows knitting together. "Please don't tell anyone I said that. I didn't mean it; I swear I didn't mean anything by it."

"Your secret's safe with me," I said. "I've slipped up a few times and called it a beauty contest myself. The girls corrected me."

"Yeah, they'll do that." She stared into the distance, lost in thought. "It's easy to forget."

It seemed there was something she wanted to tell me, so I waited with as much patience as I could muster for her to open up.

After a few minutes of staring dreamily into the waves, Susanne snapped back to earth and smiled at me. "It's just that sometimes the industry feels very *beauty* focused, don't you think?"

"Um, you mean the beauty pageant industry? Yes, I would agree."

"I know what we're *supposed* to say." Susanne crossed her arms over her chest and looked for the first time like a regular person. She wore no makeup and had a smattering of hairs plastered to her forehead from sweat. Her lips weren't blood red or plum purple, and her cheeks were flushed naturally, her freckles allowed to show on her skin. To me, she looked more attractive without the gunk caked on her face, but what did I know? That's probably why they didn't ask me to judge the pageant.

"What you're *supposed* to say?" I pressed. I had a firm recollection of interviewing Susanne at the Beauty Cottage about Mary's murder. She'd had the habit of staring off into space then, too, which was why I'd kept my questioning short. It took forever to pull a full sentence out of her.

"Yes, what I'm supposed to say," she said finally. "About how the pageant is a great opportunity for girls to win scholarships and showcase their talents and meet other women and make connections, and *yada yada*. Doesn't that sound exhausting?"

I nodded sympathetically. "Plus, you're supposed to look good while doing it. I can barely remember to put mascara on, and I definitely count cherry Chapstick as a beauty product."

"Exactly!" Susanne agreed with more life than I'd seen in her yet. "Despite all the good stuff it's supposed to do for us, at the end of the day it's still a beauty contest, isn't it? They're not picking the extra-curvy girl who's a genius at math to win anything, are they? She's just as beautiful as anyone else, inside and out."

Seemed to me Susanne had a complex. Then again, I was certain she wasn't the only one. Beauty pageants hardly seemed to be the breeding grounds for emotionally stable women.

"It's not really fair," Susanne said when she returned from her reverie. She pinched the non-existent fat around her waist. "It's not fair that the size of this or the shape of my features determines whether I'm a beautiful, successful woman."

"No, it most certainly doesn't," I agreed. "Women are

much more complex than their physical appearance — but try to get men to understand that."

"Right? *Ugh*! It's so frustrating!" She reached out a hand and smacked the tree trunk next to her. "I just wish it wasn't this way!"

The jolt of emotion was surprising. It showed me a new side of the contestant — one with passion and frustrations and problems. "Susanne, are you okay? Is something bothering you?"

"Yes! This whole stupid contest is just annoying!"

"Then why are you participating?"

She rolled her eyes. "What else am I supposed to do with my life? My mom has had me in contests since I could walk. I was four years old with crimped eyelashes and curled hair and foundation on my little baby cheeks. How messed up is that?"

"I'm sorry," I offered. "I can't imagine."

"Why the heck do you think I've taken up running?" She blew out a breath of exasperation. "My mother's here now. She wanted to stay with me — as a roommate — in the Beauty Cottage. I said no. She takes helicoptering to a new level."

"That sounds a bit overbearing," I admitted. "That would drive me insane."

"Tell me about it. Thankfully, the rules don't allow anyone except the girls competing to stay at the cottage, so she had to get a hotel room. But it doesn't stop her from dropping by any time of the day or night to make sure I popped my vitamins and curled my hair and drank my acai juice. It's ridiculous!"

"That sounds suffocating."

"You see why I run?" She shook her head. "Yes, to get away from her physically, but also as an outlet! If I didn't burn off some energy I'd explode from frustration, and that wouldn't look good on stage. No, mother wouldn't be pleased at all. She almost had a conniption when Mary was killed. Thought the show might not go on. Well, I don't think it should. What a disgrace on Edwin's part. He should have cancelled the pageant. People could've really learned something from Mary's death."

Paul had moved to sit in the hood of my rain jacket the second he'd heard footsteps approaching. It wasn't that we were ashamed of our relationship, but most people didn't quite understand why I had such a close friendship with a toad. Better if they were just left in the dark about that whole situation.

From my hood, he gave a low grumble that only I could hear. It was unnecessary, however, as I'd already been thinking about Susanne's possible involvement in the murder. Had she been frustrated enough to kill?

Having my mother hanging over my shoulder at such close quarters might drive me to insanity. Combine that with double standards and a lifetime of pressure to perform, and it was a recipe for a meltdown. It would also explain why she was so frustrated about the pageant not being cancelled — all the trouble of murder and she still hadn't gotten what she wanted?

I realized I let myself think too long because Susanne was staring curiously at me.

"Are you okay?" she asked.

"Sorry, yes. Just sympathizing. It must be a very difficult situation for you."

"Sort of," she said with a shrug. "But I guess there's nothing I can do about it."

Except kill again, a little voice in my head said, and judging by Paul's uncomfortable shift in my coat, he'd had the same thought. Yet here we were, alone in the woods, with a woman on the verge of what felt like a frustration-and-overbearing-mother-induced mental breakdown.

"Do you want me to walk you back to the cottage?" I suggested. "I can talk to Edwin if you're not feeling well enough to compete."

"And give my mother a reason to think she's right again?" she snapped. "No. I'm competing if this stupid pageant isn't cancelled. Who knows? Maybe it's not too late. Maybe Edwin will come to his senses and cancel the thing. He should be rattled more than anyone, I'd think."

"Why do you say that?"

"He just missed the murderer," she said, her lips parting in confusion. "Didn't you interview all of us? I thought you talked to Edwin."

"I did talk to Edwin, and I did interview all of the women," I said patiently, "including you. But nobody brought up Edwin just missing the murderer."

Paul gave me a poke to the back of the neck with one of his booties that told me to back off, but I didn't heed the warning. I was getting so close to overturning the one stone that could blow this whole case open. The one stone that'd cause the rest of the lies to crumble in a neat little cascade ... just like my stunt on the beach with the tower of rocks.

I gave a shudder, thinking I needed to send another note to Burt and have him get a protective detail on the Beauty Cottage in case the killer planned to strike again. Eternal Springs might not have a robust police force, but we had plenty of rent-a-cops for the shopping areas and oh-so-dangerous ritzy golf courses. It would be better than nothing.

"Susanne, I'm confused," I said. "Why didn't you tell me this when I interviewed you at the house?"

"I did," she said. "I told you I saw Edwin that morning."

"No, you didn't. I'm sorry, but I have extensive notes from all my interviews, and nobody mentioned seeing Edwin."

When she began to laugh, I wondered if she was a bit off. Her eyes flickered with recognition as she gave a cackle that sent a shiver down my spine.

"What's so funny?" I asked, forcing a smile and trying to appear lighthearted. "Are you feeling okay?"

"That's *right*," Susanne said, calming from her random bout of laughter. "I'm sorry. I told the other girl."

"The other girl?" I asked with a sinking sensation. "Did she tell you her name?"

"I think it's something like *Cloud* or *Skype*, or ... I don't know, it was one of those hippie sort of names."

I could barely hide a smile despite my disappointment. "Skye. The newspaper reporter."

"Yes, exactly. Her." Susanne poked at tugged at her lower lip in thought. "I think she must have interviewed me just before you or just after. I can't remember the order, and I guess I left out the bit about Edwin when I talked to you. It really didn't seem important, though. I mean, you don't think ... ." She looked up, horrified. "You don't think he killed Mary, do you?"

"The truth is that nobody knows who killed Mary except the killer," I said. "That's what we're trying to find out. And trust me, we will."

That last semi-threat earned another poke from Paul and his bootie. I'd have to take those shoes away when we got home. They had hard soles.

The warning from my toad was unnecessary, however, because the threat flew right over Susanne's head. She gave a shrug and looked down at her fingernails.

"Well, do you want to interview me again?" she asked. "Go ahead, though I don't think it will help. What purpose might Edwin have for murdering the star of his show?"

Even as she said it, the truth of the possibility hit us both.

It might draw attention to his show. Who knew? Maybe there'd been a personal clash between them that he'd covered up. Then he'd gone and cast suspicion on Abigail with the perfectly-timed video to distract me.

"I saw him that morning," Susanne whispered. "I was one of the only girls awake because — well, you know, I was running away from my mom. Headed out on my morning jog."

"Do you remember the time?"

"Yes. My mother called and woke me at seven twenty-four. She said she was coming to see me, so I got my butt out of bed and on the road." Susanne calculated. "It must have been around seven thirty-five."

"You don't waste time."

"It takes her nine minutes to get from the hotel to the cottage. It's a narrow window of opportunity for escape." She gave a slim smile. "When I opened the door —."

"The front door?"

"No, the back," she said, "just in case my mother was really booking it."

I thought my swallow of surprise might be audible. Even Susanne's face paled some.

"Mary was found murdered out back," she said. "You think that Edwin might have … ."

"I don't know," I said, but her surprise seemed genuine. I hadn't cut Susanne from my suspect list yet, but she moved a few notches down. Right above Mason. "I think I need to talk to him."

"Maybe that's why he's keeping the show running?" she wondered aloud. "If he did it, he could be vying for publicity or, oh, no … this is horrible. I just can't believe it."

"Don't say anything, okay?" I prompted Susanne. "We don't know if he killed her for certain. There were several other people around that morning and it's impossible to say without solid evidence."

"But it was someone," she said. "Probably someone I know."

I couldn't deny that, because for some reason I had the ugly feeling that I, too, knew the killer.

Twenty

After talking Susanne down and sending her trotting on her merry little way, I glanced one final time at the river and found it bubbling along peacefully.

That went well. You have a way of finding yourself in delightfully troubling situations, don't you?

"Delightful. You're a hoot," I told Paul. "No pressure, but now it appears we actually do have a giant slug in addition to a murderer on the loose."

I told you that already. You didn't listen.

"Consider me convinced," I said. "I think we owe the coven another chat."

Paul groaned. "Is that necessary?"

"Yes! If they can't send help, the least they can do is give me some information on what we're dealing with."

We trekked back, following the path the monster had left behind — my feet squishing through decay and sludge and broken flowers — until we reached home. I gave Bertha a wave to signal all was well. She started to ask where I'd been, but I made it up the steps and into the house before she could throw her window fully open.

I dumped Paul in the kitchen sink, plucked off his hat and booties, and then continued upstairs to the shower, where I threw the water on as hot as it would go.

It took a lot of toe tapping and impatient waiting for the room to steam up, but when there was enough condensation on the mirror to use it for finger painting I shouted for the coven to gather round.

"One moment!" Margaret appeared, covering her ears with her hands. "Jeez, Evian. We had the volume turned all the way up and now you're shouting. Relax for a second, will you?"

"I don't feel like relaxing," I said, doing a bad job at hiding my annoyance. "Then again, I don't exactly feel like fighting a giant slug back into the portal, but that's on the agenda for some reason."

"Ask the other girls for help." Margaret appeared distracted, glancing over her shoulder and waving at people behind her. Still gesturing, she turned back to me. "Skye or Kenna or Zola can help."

"I'm working on it," I said, "but they have lives too, and you know the rules. I saw him first, I have to banish him."

"Well, don't you think prioritizing the supernatural being terrorizing Eternal Springs should be high on your to-do list?"

"I suppose, but then again, I thought the coven might send some assistance," I snipped. "You seem to be against that proposal, so I'm asking for your help in determining *what* I'm dealing with. At least if I know, I stand a chance at battling the thing."

"We're ready to discuss." Margaret sighed, then thumbed behind her. "You've got about half the coven here — it was short notice and the best we could do. Describe this monster to us. And keep things brief — we're on a tight deadline."

"He's, er ... *it's* a giant slug," I said. "Purple skin — like, a *vibrant* shade of it. He appears to feed on plants and flowers and living things. However, after the creature eats, his skin gets this coating of black slime that acts like a poison. Everything he touches dies. It also appears he enjoys being in and around water."

Margaret laughed. "Just like you!"

"Will people stop comparing me to a monster?" I said. "I can't help my tendencies. So we both like *water*? We're not identical twins."

"Oh, give the little guy a break," Margaret said patiently. "He's a baby."

"Sorry, *what*?"

"I've heard of this very creature," she said, glancing at her colleagues for reassurance. Several heads bobbed in the blurry background, confirming her analysis. "You're dealing with an interesting descendent — shall we say spawn? — of Poseidon."

"That explains his love of water," I said dryly. "And some of the destruction."

"Was there a sheen to his skin?" Margaret asked. "This is very important."

"Yes, actually. A translucence that is actually quite extraordinary — Paul and I believe it makes him invisible."

"You're correct. This particular brand of magic is from the natural family of spells."

"What's that mean?"

"You have skills with water, yes?" she asked. "Tell me: Do you *think* about them or do they come naturally?"

"I think *sometimes*," I scoffed.

"Yes, but for the most part they come naturally, don't they? Water is part of who you are. The spells are easy for you. The moon pulls against you as it does the ocean. Waves dance beneath your fingers and bodies of water welcome you with open arms, so to speak."

"I suppose."

"Well, this creature's mother has a similar sort of natural magic. When her baby is born, she puts an invisibility enchantment on him for protection. It stems back to the day when magical species mixed freely with humans. Humans would hunt these creatures, so their parents formed ways to protect their offspring."

"So that giant monster is a baby?" I saw my own mystified reflection in the mirror. "That's ridiculous. It's ten feet tall and must weigh a ton!"

"Yes. When it grows to adulthood — it takes only a few months — the invisibility enchantment will fade and the purple tone of his skin will turn gray. It's easier to blend in with gray skin. However, it's imperative you banish him before he outgrows babyhood."

"I wasn't planning to keep him as a pet."

"That's not funny."

"Well, I'm asking for help to banish him!"

"At this stage of his life, the monster isn't *trying* to be destructive. He's like a human baby. He eats, sleeps ... er, excretes, and exists solely to accomplish his biological needs."

"And as he matures?"

"He develops a way of thinking. He might realize his destructive nature has power and advantages, and he'll begin to use them against you," she said. "You need to get him back through the portal as soon as possible because it might only be days until he reaches adulthood. When that happens, his invisibility is gone. Even if the monster is careful, he can't hide from everyone, and a mortal is bound to stumble across him and start asking questions."

I shuddered thinking of Buddy laying eyes on the poor slug. Even the monster didn't deserve that. "How do you recommend I get rid of him?"

"Oh, I don't know," Margaret said, unable to resist a bit of sarcasm. "I would've told you not to make bad choices and burn the school down thirteen years ago."

"I get it, you're frustrated. Still not my fault," I said. "But we won't go into that. Any *real* suggestions?"

"You know him better than us. You're both in tune with the water, so use that. He's attracted to you, or your spells — that's why he targets your garden for feeding. Though he probably won't be back now that it's a decimated mess," Margaret added. "Bertha told us it's horrible."

"Gee whiz, thanks Bertha," I mumbled. "Fine. I guess I'll be on my own then."

"Move quickly, whatever you do."

"I appreciate the encouragement. Feel free to send help."

"We have confidence in you." Margaret issued a rare smile. "Don't prove us wrong."

I shut off the shower and wiped the mirror clean, heaving with the frustration of it all. *Use your skills*, I mouthed to myself in a bad impression of Margaret. *Easier said than done.*

Not only did I need to *find* the freaking monster, then I needed to lure him to the portal and give him a little shove inside, all before Kenna shunned me for my horrible singing skills at karaoke tonight. Not an easy task.

However, something Margaret said stuck with me. *Use the other girls*. After all, weren't Skye, Kenna, Zola and myself in this together? I reviewed my previous plan to beg Zola for help and decided it was the best option. After all, it'd been great to have backup the time we found ourselves mid-removal of a murderous mermaid from the beach. I would've lost a finger if Kenna and Skye hadn't shoved her off me in time.

Maybe if I created a trail bursting with blooming flowers and a pinch of magic I could sucker Bob — my shortened name for the creature — into following the trail to the portal.

I had the water spells and surely Zola could hook me up with some plants. All I needed was a good bribe.

Buzzing with the ease of my plan, I ran downstairs and found Paul sitting in an empty margarita glass, waiting for me to fill it to the brim with his favorite strawberry blend.

"I know what to do," I told Paul. "Your bath will have to wait."

Give me a bath or I'll tell the coven you hid from their call last week. I covered for you, but I will snitch.

I sighed, pulled out the blender, and threw in the ingredients for a double margarita. With an extra dose of attitude, I picked up the glass and sent Paul flying as I flipped it over, dusted it with lime juice and dipping it in sugar. Pouring the mixture into the righted glass, I gave a huff of relief.

"There. Are you happy?"

Ah. He climbed into the frothy beverage and stuck his front two feet behind his head. *This is the life.*

Twenty-One

With Paul basking happily in his margarita, I slung my rain jacket on and hurried down to Zola's garden shop. Due to the festivities this evening, most residents of Eternal Springs were busy getting dolled up for the karaoke event or gossiping behind closed doors, which left Cackleberries mercifully empty.

"Hi," I said, leaning against the counter and gasping for breath. "Slow day today, huh?"

Zola frowned. "What do you need this time?"

"I can't just swing by to say hello?"

"Is that what you're doing?"

"No," I admitted. "I have a problem."

Satisfied, Zola stuck a hip against the counter and pulled her gardening gloves off. "What'd you do this time?"

"I didn't *do* anything," I said. "Let me remind you that someone — one of us — was lazy thirteen years ago and allowed the portal to open, which is why we have Bob."

"Bob?"

"The giant slug. Paul was right," I told her. "I just got off the mirror with the coven, and the members agree. He's some weird spawn of Poseidon, and I have to get him back through the portal before he matures into adulthood."

"So, what, you have a few years?"

"Days? Hours?" I shrugged my shoulders. "Nobody knows, but I've been warned not to keep him as a pet. I think things get nasty when the slug develops hormones and a brain."

"Don't we all," Zola said with a sigh. "Well, all right then. What do you need from me?"

"All of your extra plants."

"My extra plants?"

"Living things," I clarified. "I don't care if they're half dead and ready for the compost pile, I need anything with a bit of life left in it."

She frowned. "I sell most of my plants, Evian. That's how I make a living."

"Something, anything? I need to make a trail to the portal with them. He likes to eat living things, and he's drawn to the magic in my watering spell," I said. "It's a full moon tonight. It's the perfect time to capture him."

"I told you, I don't have a ton of extra plants, and you're not taking my live and healthy ones."

I glanced around the garden and spotted a huge pile of compost and dirt and fading greenery. "What about those?"

"We just weeded the gardens, those are ... ." She hesitated, glancing over to me with a new sparkle in her eye. "You think that slug of yours can differentiate between beautiful flowers and weeds?"

"Judging by his taste in skin color, probably not," I said, equally giddy. "It's worth a shot! Can I have at 'em?"

"I'll throw in a few extra healthy plants to spice things up," Zola said. "Consider it my donation to the good of the island."

"I owe you big time. Thank you so much."

"I know how you can repay me," Zola said with a twinkling smile. "How about a little of that magical watering spell you have up your sleeve? My gardens could use a good dosing."

I groaned. "I can only do it under the full moon."

"Great," Zola said. "Then I'll see you here tonight. Now, shall we get started?"

Zola and I made so many trips to and from the path that the wheelbarrow wore deep grooves into the ground and kept getting stuck. We'd both nearly twisted an ankle more times than we could count, but thankfully we'd escaped without serious injury.

"There," Zola said as we dumped the last wheelbarrow full of weeds and other greenery in a winding path that led directly to the portal. "I think that should be enough. Will it work?"

"I don't know." I wiped a sleeve across my forehead and looked over the horizon where the sun had begun to set. Already the moon had risen in the pale blue sky. "I sure hope so, because I don't have any other options."

The path of plants we created had the potential to draw the monster out of his hiding place, wherever that might be. Fresh-cut flowers crisscrossed with flourishing swatches of dandelions, interspersed with rows of herbs. Zola had donated some small fruit trees that probably wouldn't last the year as an especially tasty treat near the mouth of the portal to seal the deal.

Heading back to the grounds of our former school wasn't exactly a pleasant experience, but a necessary one. St. Joan of

Arc had been a place for burgeoning witches to spend time learning their craft, experience high school and generally dog things human teenagers did, save for the whole magical element.

"Try your full-moon spell," Zola encouraged. "I've never actually seen you use it."

"I can't yet. It's not dark."

"But the moon's out!"

I grinned as Zola pointed upward. It wasn't the traditional "shining by the light of the moon" lauded in songs, but it might be enough. "Doesn't hurt to try, I suppose. If it doesn't take I can come back when the sun sets."

Zola gave an encouraging nod. "Exactly. It's not as if the fate of Eternal Springs rests on your shoulders or anything."

I closed my eyes and blocked out the distractions. I took my time envisioning the length of the winding, twisting bed of plants we'd created — plants that had a touch of magic in their stems, having been cared for by Zola — and felt the flow of life, of magic, through it. If anything, Bob would find our trap even more tantalizing because of the duality of my water magic joining with Zola's earth tendencies.

Next, I concentrated on the clouds, filtering through the mess of a storm that'd been kept at bay for the last few hours. I played lightly with the tenuous spattering of precipitation in the clouds, envisioning droplets of dainty rain falling in an isolated line over Zola's plants. I merged the two magics and, when I felt ready, I invoked the spell: "Sprinkle water by the new full moon; then watch your garden grow and bloom!"

When I opened my eyes, my first glimpse was of Zola's face — and her jaw hanging wide open. I followed her gaze, pride blooming as I watched a light, delicate spattering of rain drip onto the flowers, seep into the ground and absorb into the newly-rooted plants.

"Well, if that doesn't work," I said, turning to Zola, "I'm

out of options. I'll swing back after karaoke tonight. Speaking of, have you decided which song to sing?"

Zola winced at me. "Is there an option to *not* sing?"

"Let's give Kenna all our slots," I suggested, "to save the ears of the general public. You think she'd go for it?"

"Not a chance."

Twenty-Two

"*W*hat is *loooove?*" I wailed into my hairbrush. "Baby, don't hurrrt me —."

What is that noise? Paul had basked in his margarita bath all afternoon, pulling himself out of it only once he'd licked all the sugar from the rim of the glass and digested the tequila. He hiccupped. *You sound like a dying cow. I bet Bob can sing better than you.*

"Well, we won't know until we find Bob now, will we?" I said, holding up one dress in front of my body and then switching it out for another. "Which do you prefer?"

What do you think I am, your stylist? Paul burped. *Go with the red. It's sexy.*

I wrinkled my nose. "Please remove the word 'sexy' from your vocabulary. And that's the last time I'll put two shots of tequila into your beverage."

He turned his toad lips into a pout. *Why can't toads be sexy?*

I didn't grace his drunken slur with an answer. "You don't like my song?"

The song is fine. It's your voice that's breaking my ears.

"Fine, then stay home tonight."

Fine, Paul retorted. *Can I get a hot tub in a bath of red wine?*

"No. You're cut off."

But —.

"Paul, no." I pointed my finger at him like I might a petulant child. "I know you're not all brave and whatnot, but I might need you to watch my back tonight after karaoke."

In case someone tries to murder you for breaking their eardrums?

"Ha-ha, not funny. A murderer is on the loose, and I'm hunting monsters. Keep joking, Paul, and I'll feed you to Bob."

You aren't real clever with names, Paul mused as he flopped on his back inside one of my high heels. It was the perfect little chaise style lounger for him. *Paul and Bob aren't winning any awards for originality, are they?*

"Good. *Bye.*" I slammed my foot into my shoe, just narrowly avoiding squashing Paul's toes. "Be the watch-frog for me."

I'm a toad.

"Yeah, and watch-toad doesn't sound as cool," I said. "How do I look? Be honest. But not too honest."

Paul scampered to a better vantage point atop his dresser and studied me from head to toe. *You look nice, Evian.*

"Okay, be more honest than that."

Paul's eyes looked extra watery, and I wondered if toads experienced emotional rollercoasters when intoxicated, much like some humans. *You look really beautiful, Evian. If that moron Mason is there tonight, he'd better ask you to dance.*

"Stop lying to me. Is my hair —?"

I'm not lying. You look great. I hope you have some fun — you deserve it.

"Fat chance," I said. "Kenna always makes us sing, and I'd rather have a mermaid bite off all my toes one by one."

Paul nodded. *Shame I can't sing for you. They say I have a real deep, throaty voice.*

"I'm sure it's beautiful, Paul. Sleep it off." I gave my toad a lift downstairs to his porch bed. After shutting off lights and locking the door, I gave Bertha a wave as I stepped outside.

She promptly dropped her binoculars. Then, the window came up. "Is that you, Evian?"

"Yes, Bertha," I replied patiently. "Who else would it be?"

This was our little song and dance every time I came out of the house looking like a fancier version of myself. Thank heavens I didn't date much or Bertha would have a bruised toe from dropping the binoculars on herself. Apparently I managed to look enough of a slouch that even a little hairspray and lipstick counted as a disguise.

"You're not going to Coconuts?" I called. "I hear you were a real siren back in your day."

"This old hip ain't working right," Bertha said. "Plus, sometimes I think I can hear the music from here."

More likely, Bertha didn't feel like fighting Kenna for the microphone. Not that I blamed her. If I was old and could pull off the whole agoraphobic excuse as well as Bertha I might never leave the house, either.

I puttered down the path, picking my way carefully. Due to the high heels, my walk to Coconuts was longer than usual.

"May I walk you to the show?"

A distinctly male voice caught me off guard and my klutz mode enabled. I took a step, a skip, and then I toppled headfirst into the bushes. A hand reached out to help me up, but I pushed it aside and fought the bottom of my dress to stay down as I reloaded myself back onto my stilettos.

"Mason," I said, as I tried to regain normal breathing patterns after my wipeout. "What's up?"

"I'm so sorry." His expression had worked itself into one of true remorse. "I didn't mean to startle you. Are you okay? Did you hurt anything? You must have twisted an ankle in those shoes."

"Nope, I'm used to falling in them," I said cheerfully, fighting off my wave of embarrassment with a fake grin. "Put them on and *whoops*! Timber, if you know what I mean."

"Then why do you wear them?"

"Societal pressure. And Kenna."

"Look, I know this is probably inappropriate timing considering that I just about bowled you over, but you really do look gorgeous, Evian. Stunning."

My flush grew hotter. "Thanks. I should, ah, probably get a move on, though, or Kenna's head will light on fire. She doesn't like when I'm late."

"Who cares what Kenna thinks?"

I almost asked him to marry me then and there. He did have a point. "Er — it's complicated."

"May I walk with you?" He extended a hand. "If you'd prefer, I can give you a piggy back ride. I owe you one after sending you into the bushes."

I fought back the weird giggle bubbling up from my stomach. Giving a cockeyed nod, I let him slip his arm through mine and drag me along toward Coconuts.

The road was mostly empty. Most people were probably at the bar already, fighting for a place on the singing roster that I'd gratefully give up if I had the choice. With my luck, Kenna had already signed me up. Maybe I could pawn it off on someone else.

"Say, do you want to sing tonight?" I asked Mason.

He frowned. "Together? I did say I owed you one, so I guess ... ."

"Oh — er, I meant, I hate singing. Kenna might try to force me to, however, and I will happily give you my spot."

"In that case, no thanks. I'd rather watch you flounder." He winked. "I'm also wondering if maybe we can stop talking about Kenna for a second and talk about us."

"Us?"

"You. Me," he said. "Have you thought about what I said at all? Are you any closer to finding the murderer? I hate to sound impatient, but I'd really love to take you out, Evian."

"Why me?"

"What do you mean, *why* you?"

"I mean," I started, already feeling the heat rush up the back of my neck, "why are you asking me out on a date? It's no secret your roster of ex-girlfriends is as long as the karaoke list at Coconuts tonight."

"Not quite."

"Fine, but you get the picture." I sighed. "My point is that you could ask anyone on this island out on a date, but here you are helping me out of the bushes."

"I wouldn't be helping you out if I hadn't made you fall in." He gave a smile, but it was a lopsided one that lasted but a second. When it faded, he watched me out of the corner of his eye. "There are so many reasons I'm interested in you."

"Which is more appealing? The fact that I trip over my own feet or the fact that my toad says I sound like a dying cow when I sing?"

He blinked. "Your toad?"

"Oh. Er, yeah," I said, struggling to cover up for my slip. Usually I was good about keeping my mouth shut about Paul, but I was flummoxed by Mason's grip on my arm. "It was a joke. Though I do have a toad. Named Paul. Long story. Anyway, you wanted to talk about us?"

"Let's talk about you." Mason stopped moving and shifted his body so we were face to face. "Evian, you're friendly. You're fun, and you make me laugh, and every day that I see you is a little brighter day than all the others."

As if on cue, the moon's glow shone clearly down on us, casting lengthy shadows in every direction while encasing us in light. "Mason, I didn't mean you had to talk about me. I'm just curious about why me and not someone more ... stable?"

"Because I'm not interested in anyone else," he said. "We might not know each other all that well yet, but I know it's something I'd like to explore. Of course you're beautiful and I love your smile, but that's just superficial. You make me feel happier, and I can't explain why."

I gave an awkward laugh. "You make me feel happier too."

"I'm not saying you have to fall in love with me, Evian. I just thought it'd be fun to get dinner together. We can take things slow."

"But Mary ... ."

"I know you don't have a reason to trust me yet, so I'm not going to push you," he said, raising a hand to brush a drooping curl from my face. "But I hope for my selfish sake, and for Mary's, that this case gets wrapped up quickly so I can buy you a plate of tacos."

Though I'd tried to keep my guard up, something about the tone of Mason's voice had me melting on the inside like an ice cube. I really, really didn't want Mason to be Mary's murderer. Maybe it was the magic of the full moon, or maybe I was finally opening to trying out something new, but this felt right, and I didn't want this moment to end.

"I suppose we should get on, as you said." He broke the silence, nodding toward Coconuts, where the music had grown in volume. "Now, tell me more about this toad."

I shook my head and gave him a completely fabricated story about how I'd caught Paul along with Kenna, Skye and Zola back at school. It wasn't all false, I supposed, and there was enough truth to have both of us laughing by the end of it.

"So, are you allowed to date?" Mason asked, an air of stiffness to his words. "You know, what with your history and all?"

"My history?"

"The school — weren't you set on becoming a nun or something?"

"Er, sort of," I said, wishing the creators had thought up a different lie — anything else. I would've rather had a fake mortician profile as my background. "But I'm not and that's what matters. Moving along."

"Tell me about —."

"Actually," I interrupted as we came upon the bar. "I'm really sorry, Mason, can I join you inside in a few minutes?"

"Is it something I said? The whole nun thing really doesn't bother me," he said. "So long as, you know, it's in the past."

"No, no — I just ... ." I nodded my head toward the back entrance to Coconuts, where a figure sat in the shadows. "I want to pay my condolences to Edwin before I find Kenna."

Mason's brow furrowed. "I'll wait here for you."

"Maybe put my name down on the karaoke list?"

"I thought you hated singing."

"Buy me a drink?" I said. "I'm sorry. I'd just prefer privacy. It's a sensitive subject."

He bowed his head, looking not quite convinced, but gave a firm nod. "I'll see you inside, Evian. Be careful."

His warning seemed out of place, but somehow warranted. I watched as Mason disappeared into the bar. Once he passed the bouncers on duty, I made my move.

Turning my back on the party, I snuck around to the dark alley behind the festivities to find Edwin. Apparently the beauty pageant coordinator had a habit of sneaking off to places he shouldn't. All I needed was confirmation he'd seen Mary the morning of the murder and finally, I suspected, the puzzle would come together.

Twenty-Three

"Having a smoke?" I asked, feeling dumb the second the words came out of my mouth. Of course Edwin was having a smoke. A cigarette was pressed to his lips and its toxic fumes were marching straight up my nostrils.

He raised his eyebrow in answer. "Aren't you Encyclopedia Brown."

I gave a pointed cough. "Smoking can kill you."

"So can murder," he said. "Did you want something?"

I gulped. "Actually, I'm terribly sorry to interrupt." I gestured to the empty alley behind the bar. "It looks like you're very busy, but I do have a question for you."

"I answered all of your questions already."

"Right, but according to a source, you got one answer wrong."

"What are you talking about?"

"You told me you were dealing with 'that stupid K-cup machine' at the time of Marilyn's murder."

"Yep, again, Sherlock"

"I'm fairly certain you lied about that, considering I have

two eyewitnesses that place you at the crime scene just around the time of Mary's murder."

The cocky smirk was wiped clean off his face. "Who snitched on me?"

"That's not exactly a denial now, is it?" I crossed my arms. "What were you doing there?"

"I don't have to answer your questions."

"No, but it looks mighty bad if you don't."

"The police haven't expressed doubt in my story, so while I am flattered by your obsession with me, I have no interest in engaging with you."

"Just talk to me."

"That would be engaging." Edwin took the cigarette from his lips and pressed it out with a hiss against the cool cement wall. "Have fun at the party."

I closed my eyes as Edwin leaned in and blew a smoky breath right at my face. I did my best to seal my lips and nose to avoid the musty scent of him as he stalked off, and I held my breath until I reached fresh air.

By the time I'd resumed normal lung activity, Edwin had disappeared. I followed his path toward the front door, thinking that our brief interaction had shown me a more colorful side of the pageant coordinator. Obviously he was hiding something about his visit to the Beauty Cottage on the morning of the murder. If he had simply been checking up on the girls, why not say so?

"Don't you dare say anything about our talk." Edwin surprised me, blocking my entrance to the bar with a quick sidestep. He'd been waiting in the shadows for me to round the corner. "I didn't kill Mary."

"Why don't I believe you?"

"Look, I had a few questions for the girls that morning and I was just there to check up on them."

"Why didn't you say so from the start? You had to imagine one of the girls would see you."

His cheeks turned pink. "I tried to be careful."

"You weren't careful enough. Several people saw you."

"Fine," he snapped. "The truth is that I ran into Mary at the cottage. We chatted in the backyard for a few minutes, and then I left."

"If you were there to check on the girls, why didn't you go into the cottage?" I struggled for Edwin's explanation to make sense, but nothing was clicking. "I don't understand why any of this had to be a secret if you're innocent."

"How would it look if I was there talking to Mary a few minutes before she was murdered?"

"It looks a lot worse now that you lied."

"That's not what I mean. I'm talking about our ... ." He trailed off, peering at my face. "Forget it. Yes, I was there that morning. I ran into Mary, we had a chat and I left. It was stupid Susanne who saw me, wasn't it? The psychotic runner chick?"

"She's not psychotic, and you'd be a runner too if your mother hung over your shoulder watching your every move," I said, feeling defensive. "And this is not about Susanne, so don't go punishing her. She wasn't tattling on you — she didn't even suspect you did anything wrong. All she did was mention running past you when she left that morning. You're the one who's turning this into a whole big thing."

"It's not a *whole big thing*," he snapped. "Leave it alone."

Edwin closed the conversation by slipping past the bouncers. Unfortunately, I had to stop and show my ID, which meant that by the time I eased into Coconuts he had long since vanished into the crowd.

Kenna should be happy, I thought, coming to a stop just inside to the door. *Everyone* was here. If anything, murder was good for tourism — though nobody should tell Kenna that. She was so enthusiastic about her director of the tourism board position that she might just poison a few of her enemies to get annual visit counts up. I'm kidding, of course — m*ostly*.

I scanned the bar and took stock of the hustle and bustle. Abigail, of course, was up on stage with her breasts pressed to her chin and her dress hugging her hips, belting out some unintelligible song and gyrating her hips.

"That's our medical examiner, ladies and gents," Skye whispered in my ear as she slid next to me. "Dang if Eternal Springs shouldn't be proud."

"You know, I actually don't mind her up there," I said, trying to keep a straight face. "The longer she swings those hips, the longer I have to fight off Kenna."

"Then put your boxing gloves on," Skye advised. "We're up next."

"What? No!" Panic instantly flooded my chest. "No, that's impossible. I'm not mentally prepared. What song? What is this *we* business?"

"Kenna organized a little tribute for Mary. She wants everyone in the bar to dissolve into tears." Skye rolled her eyes. "Not exactly the way to liven up a party, if you ask me."

"Someone needs to get control of that witch."

Skye laughed. "I'm just warning you. I call the dysfunctional microphone."

"No, that one's mine! You know I always choose that one!" I hated pleading with Skye, but it was worth it for the dud microphone. "I need the broken one because if people actually hear me sing, they might die."

Skye shrugged. "More murders equates to more ratings for your show, more readers for my newspaper and more visitors for the tourism board. Don't tell Kenna, though, or she'll begin offing us all."

"I had that same thought!" My face felt caught between a laugh and gaping horror. "It's awful, isn't it?"

Skye glanced my way. "I know you're not used to covering such tragic things what with your fluff job, but you can't take everything so personally. Take it from me, the expert."

"Skye, you report on the opening of new ice cream shops and the mowing of the median."

"I had that one concussion I did a story on, and what about the theft of Bernie's button?"

"Hi, what are we talking about?" Zola asked as she joined us. "Tell me Kenna didn't rope us into doing some stupid song. By the way, any news on Bob?"

"Bob?" Skye asked. "What have I missed?"

I filled them both in on the story of Bob the Slug, and then continued on to the rest of my afternoon. Just when I was getting to my odd interaction with Edwin in the alley, Kenna found the three of us with our heads together and wedged her long skinny nose into the party.

"So," she said. "What's the gossip?"

"Evian has a pet monster named Bob," Skye summarized, "and she's going to kill people with her singing."

"What?" Kenna took a deep breath. It appeared she'd taken up yoga or something because she managed to keep her voice somewhat calm. "I'm not going to ask because I don't want to know. No killing people, all right? And leave Bob out of this. We have a tribute to focus on."

"Whatever you say, captain," I said with a salute that brought a smile to Skye's face. Zola turned away, probably hiding a similar expression that seemed lost on Kenna.

"Get your rear ends on stage. After Little Miss Elvis gets done grinding with herself up there," Kenna said, thumbing over her shoulder, "we're up. I have a short announcement and then I'll flick the song on."

"What song?" My heart thumped a panicky sort of beat.

"I really think I should watch and cheer from down here. Maybe I can get the clapping started? Or what about the tambourine? I think that might make a nice accent."

"If I'm dragged up there," Zola said, "you're dragged up there. No exceptions."

Skye agreed with a nod and Kenna cemented it with a smirk of her own.

"Then that's settled," she said. "I'll see you onstage."

"I'm getting a drink," Skye said, and Zola doubled it by holding up two fingers. "Yeah, all right," Skye amended. "Let's make that a few drinks. Evian, you coming with us?"

"Er — not now. In a minute," I said. "I'll — don't worry about me."

"Don't you dare sneak out on us," Skye said, "or I'll blow you into the mainland and Kenna will burn the ends of your hair. Do you remember when she did that to me? You don't want that, trust me."

"No." I shuddered, recalling Skye's horrifying hairdo after she'd offended Kenna's organizational skills. "I just have to say hi to someone."

The truth was that I'd seen Billie Jo enter the bar, and as she was both a familiar face and a resident of the Beauty Cottage, at this point she might be my best option to procure a few more details about Edwin. Even if she didn't have the answers, she might know who did. It was obvious she took pride in knowing everything and everyone at the cottage, so I said a quick prayer to the water gods that she'd be in a chatty mood tonight.

Chatty she was, I realized, the second I touched her shoulder. Her eyes were just a bit unfocused and her words came out a little too loudly.

"Billie Jo, are you feeling okay?" I asked. "You seem off balance."

She giggled in a high-pitched whine and took a tottering

step toward me. "Some of the other girls and I shared a bottle of wine to get ready for tonight. We thought we'd need the courage, you know?"

"Courage for what?"

"Oh, the tribute and whatnot. That anal-retentive organizer of yours —."

"Kenna?"

"Yeah, that one. She came over and gave us the rundown of the evening in a minute-by-minute itinerary. She told us we couldn't miss the tribute because we'd all bawl our eyes out."

"Oh, Kenna. I'll talk to her, Billie Jo. And I'm sorry. I promise you she only meant well. She wanted to recognize Mary for all of her successes and the wonderful person she was."

"No, no ... ." Billie Jo raised a finger and tried to smoosh it against my lips, but she missed and nearly clawed my nostril. "I'm just saying it's sad. I think the tribute is nice. Just don't tell her that a few of us are four sheets to the wind."

"I think you mean three sheets, Billie Jo."

She held up her fingers and made a serious effort to count. "One, two ... ." She paused, stuck up two fingers to make four. "*Three?* You're right."

I patted her head. "Say, I think we should get you a water and a seat. Come over here, sweetie."

I led Billie Jo to a table, elbowing out some kids who looked as though they'd used fake IDs to get into the bar. They barely grunted with annoyance. As they moved, they didn't bother to break eye contact with Abigail's chest. If there was anything good about our medical examiner, it was her ability to distract a crowd.

"Okay," I said, sitting down next to Billie Jo. "Drink this, and then eat this. You'll feel better."

I grabbed a fresh basket of bread from an older couple at the table next to us who didn't notice — they were also transfixed on Abigail — and I wrestled a dinner roll into Billie Jo's hand.

She took a bite and grinned. "Yum."

"I know, it's gourmet," I said. "It's also probably been weeks since you've eaten carbs."

"Months," she corrected. "Stupid beauty pageant."

"Exactly. And speaking of the stupid beauty pageant, I need to ask you something about Edwin."

She wrinkled her nose. "Okay."

"Did you see him the morning of Mary's murder?" When she shook her head no, I continued. "Some girls saw him at the cottage. He admitted he talked to Mary. I'm wondering if you know what that might have been about."

She began to laugh so hard she choked, and I had to clap her on the back and watch as a crumb of bread flew into a neighbor's drink.

"Sorry," I said, before the man could get angry. "I'll buy you a new one."

He frowned and handed his drink off to a passing waiter while barely interrupting his gaze at Abigail. This was the most I'd ever liked the woman.

"Did you find something funny?" I prodded Billie Jo, whose gaze had wandered in the short amount of time I'd been distracted. "Something about Edwin and Mary? Was there something going on between the two?"

"He *wishes*."

I blinked, the shock settling over me in waves. "What do you mean, 'He wishes?'"

"He's been asking her out for months! I swear, he invites her to dinner, like, once a week." Tears popped into Billie Jo's eyes, though whether from sadness or humor, I couldn't tell. "I'm just glad she got to reject him one more time before she died. What a creep."

"Did Edwin do anything else ... ." I searched for the word and couldn't find a good one. "Er, creeptastic?"

She shrugged. "I think repeatedly asking out a woman in the pageant he's coordinating is creepy. But that was the extent of it as far as I'm concerned."

"Did Mary ever ... ."

"Oh, no. She would have never gone out with him." Billie's eyelashes fluttered. "As far as I knew, she was single, but she also wasn't looking — and she *especially* wasn't looking at him."

I followed Billie Jo's nod to Edwin, who stood sulking in the corner. As much as I wanted to go over there and really give him something to sulk about, I'd accomplish more by getting to the bottom of this murder. If Edwin had gotten angry and killed Mary, he needed to pay for it — before his temper got the better of him again.

"You're sure she wasn't seeing anyone?"

"I'm not sure," Billie Jo revised with a nonchalant shrug. "I mean, she could have been, but it would have been near impossible."

"Why's that?"

"First of all, it's hard to hide stuff in the cottage. Everyone knows everyone's business. And she was never making phone calls, writing notes or sneaking away to spend time with anyone. She was focused on her career and on getting that sixtieth win." Billie's eyes genuinely watered up this time. "Poor thing. All her time was spent training with Carl, exercising or practicing the piano. Whatever time she had left was for beauty rest. Really, the girl barely got to socialize. I don't see how she could've possibly taken a lover on the side."

"Plus all the travel," I agreed. "I don't know how any of you would be able to sustain a relationship. I haven't dated forever, and I have none of those excuses."

"Yeah, but he hasn't taken his eyes off you since you got in here." Billie's head bobbed dangerously close to the table as she nodded at Mason. "You should go say hi."

"Thanks, Billie Jo, but I might —."

Her head hit the table with a light thunk, and the snores followed shortly after.

"Oh, boy," I said, just as Kenna pulled herself up on stage and shooed Abigail off after her fourth standing ovation. I couldn't leave an unconscious girl alone in a bar per the general female safety code, so I glanced around, looking for one of her friends. Most of the other girls were either chatting with someone or looking in danger of a snoozefest themselves.

"Need some help?"

In my haste to find someone to watch Billie Jo, I'd missed Mason's evacuation of his seat and journey across the room. Turning, I found him standing next to the table with a blasé smile on his face.

"I can play babysitter if you need," he said. "She'll be safe with me. We'll just sit here together until you're done."

I nodded gratefully. "Thank you so much. Kenna apparently is making us do this tribute, and —."

"I'm looking forward to it." Mason sat in the chair next to Billie Jo and shooed me away. "Go on. I can't wait to see this."

Kenna's gaze was just about burning holes in my head by the time I reached the stage and joined my other fake-nun sisters.

"About time," Kenna snapped. "Where were you?"

"Doesn't matter," I said, grabbing for the janky microphone in Skye's hand. "Please? I don't even know what song we're singing!"

"*Dancing Queen*," Kenna said. "But replace 'Dancing' with 'Beauty.' You know, *Beauty Queen, young and sweet* ... ."

"Oh, jeez," I said. "Are you serious?"

"It's creative," Kenna insisted. "The other girls think so too. Right, ladies?"

I used the moment of awkward silence to snatch the dysfunctional mic from Skye's hand and replace it with the working one. The entire bar would be better for it.

Before Skye could react, the music started. I dodged her ensuing lunge and tiptoed to the other side of the stage. The slight flare of flame in Kenna's hair silenced us just in time for the lyrics to kick into full swing.

We launched into the song, performing the most awkward combination of song and dance known to Eternal Springs. I was just preparing a suicidal stage dive when I caught sight of Mason's whimsical smile in the audience. He looked as if he wasn't quite sure whether he should be horrified or intrigued at what was happening on stage, and I didn't blame him one bit.

One glance at the rest of the crowd told me that Kenna's short speech in tribute to Mary had worked wonders. People were wiping damp eyes and heaving sobs onto friends' shoulders. Either that or we were bad enough at karaoke to make the entire crowd cry. I wouldn't put it past my singing voice to bring tears to a person's eyes — especially after I'd made Paul weep with my hairbrush solo earlier in the afternoon.

Halfway through the song, I glimpsed movement near the door. I paused my lip-syncing to watch as Edwin moved quickly to the bouncers, spoke to them under his breath, and then slipped into the night. His shoulders were hunched, his eyes downcast, as if he'd seen something — or someone — that'd spooked him. After what I'd just heard from Billie Jo about his intentions with Mary, my hackles stood to attention.

My gut told me that he was preparing to run. I'd already lost one of my prime suspects to the ferry; I wouldn't lose a second — especially not Puff-the-Magic-Dragon-in-my-face Edwin.

"Sorry," I called to the other witches above the music. "I've got urgent business."

I thrust the faulty microphone into Skye's hand and tried my best to slip off stage unnoticed. From the bar, I felt Mason's eyes follow me, but he couldn't in good conscience leave Billie Jo alone after he'd promised to watch over her. Just like the other singing witches couldn't yell at me in the middle of the song. As a matter of fact, I'd picked the perfect time to leave ... though I'd pay for it later.

As I raced between the tables in pursuit of Edwin I found myself hoping Kenna would feel forgiving and avoid singeing the edges of my hair. I already had unruly dead ends. Fuzzy tips would just make everything horrid, especially in this humidity.

The bouncers parted to let me barrel through. I launched from the bar into the darkness that had fallen and hesitated, feeling the wash of moonlight splash on my face. The full moon had officially arrived, which meant my powers would be at their strongest. So would Bob's, but monster hunting had been put on the backburner until after karaoke.

Edwin was nowhere in sight, but I careened around the corner and found myself hurtling toward the back alley. I couldn't quite say why I felt the rush, the urgency, save for the fact that the entire evening had started with a single thread pulled when Susanne had mentioned Edwin's name. The mystery had begun to unravel as I followed that string, and things felt close to a tipping point. One little nudge and the whole web of lies would come tumbling down.

"Edwin," I gasped pulling to a stop in the alley. "What are you doing?"

He raised a lazy hand and gestured to the cigarette

drooping from his fingers. "The same thing I was doing the last time you assaulted me."

"I didn't ... ." I hesitated, the sound of soft sobs coming from further down the alley. "Is someone else out here?"

Edwin rolled his eyes. "Apparently the tribute hit Carl right in *the feels*. I came out here to check on him, but he doesn't want to talk."

I stepped a few feet further down the alley, where I found Carl huddled on an abandoned set of filthy steps that led nowhere. Normally, I would have sat next to him and offered a one-armed hug, but there was no way I was ruining my nice dress on that filth. The man could stand up if he wanted a hug that badly. Plus, in these heels, it'd be a miracle if I ever stood up again after sitting down.

"Carl, what's wrong?"

"You have to ask?" he moaned. "Weren't you in there? Didn't you listen to Kenna talk about Mary during the tribute? And now she's gone. *Forever*. We'll never win that sixtieth crown together."

"It's not only about the winning," I said. "I mean, it's sad she's gone because — oh, you know — she's a *person*."

Carl turned away from me and continued sobbing. I wanted to help the man, but he growled for me to get away from him. He seemed more upset with the loss of a crown than the loss of a life. Poor Mary. For that matter, poor Susanne. Poor Tarryn and Billie Jo and the whole lot of them. They were nothing but show toys for the rest of the world.

"I need to talk to you." I confronted Edwin, keeping my voice low as I left Carl to cry. "You ditched out on our conversation before. I wasn't done talking to you."

"We're done. I asked you not to say anything." His eyes flashed in anger. "You don't know what you're dealing with — you should have listened to me and stayed out of this."

Hopefully Edwin wouldn't commit murder — possibly for

a second time — with Carl crying into his rumrunner on the disgusting steps. I felt vaguely more comfortable that we had a witness, though Carl's eyes were so red he was probably seeing double and wouldn't be considered reliable in court. Not that I'd be around to see the outcome, if Edwin got to me first.

"It just so happens I heard another little spin on your story in the bar," I told Edwin. "You asked Mary out repeatedly?"

Edwin's back stiffened. His fingers pinched the cigarette so tightly the ashes fell to the ground. I stepped back to avoid them getting on my shoes and gave a frustrated wrinkle of my nose.

"Where'd you hear that?" He hissed. "I told you not to dig deeper into this, Evian. What makes you think this is your business?"

"It's not my business, it's Mary's," I said. "And she deserves justice. She can't get it for herself, so I'm trying to help. You killed her, didn't you?"

The crying stopped. Carl seemed to be listening intently, which didn't stop me from pressing onward. The more witnesses the better, especially because I hadn't thought ahead to what I might actually do when Edwin inevitably admitted his guilt.

"You went over there to ask Mary to dinner and she refused — *again*. Isn't that right?" I asked. "And isn't it right that you just so happen to *hate* getting rejected? I mean, we all do, but not all of us commit murder over it."

"It's not like that."

"You got upset — maybe reached out and found your hands around her neck. When you squeezed, you began to see how easy it might be to go for just a second longer ... ." I paused. "Was it an accident? Did you tussle, and then she fell into the pool and drowned? Or were you trying to disguise it as an accident?"

"You." Carl rose to his feet, his gaze murderous. "You killed *my* Marilyn?"

"*Your* Marilyn?!" I spun around. "Wait a second. What's going on here?"

"I didn't kill anyone." Edwin raised his hands and let the cigarette drop to the ground. "If you're looking for a murder of passion, look no further than that man. They were lovers. Mary admitted it to me the day she died. I hadn't known she was a taken woman or I never would have asked her out in the first place."

"Why'd you ask her out so many times?"

"I don't know! I liked her. I thought she was special," Edwin said. "And I thought she was single. But the whole time she'd been rejecting me for him. Carl!"

"Is that true?" I turned to Carl. "Were you in a relationship with Marilyn?"

"I loved her!" Carl growled, inching toward Edwin. "You killed her, didn't you? She told you we were in a relationship that morning so you'd leave her alone."

"I thought you were married," I said to Carl. "What about your wife?"

"She divorced him a year ago," Edwin said with a smirk. "She left him for a younger man."

"I didn't want to be divorced," Carl said. "I loved my wife and had always been faithful to her. She left me a year and a half ago, served me divorce papers six months later. Marilyn and I didn't start up until three months ago, so yes, she was my girlfriend."

"But which one of you killed her?" I muttered this mostly to myself, but apparently it was loud enough for them to hear because they simultaneously pointed to one another and declared the other party guilty.

"I went to the cottage to go over some plans with the girls," Edwin said. "Mary confronted me out back and said she wanted to talk. She apologized for not being honest sooner about the reasons she'd rejected me and then explained about her relationship with Carl and why they'd wanted to keep it a secret."

"And then you killed her!" Carl shouted. "Out of jealousy!"

"Of course I didn't, you buffoon," Edwin said. "I was surprised, yes. Maybe upset, but I turned around and left. I didn't feel up to discussing plans with the girls, which is why I called a formal meeting the next day to go over that same itinerary. Next thing I knew, *this one* had stumbled over the body. I kept quiet because I knew how bad things looked for me."

"You should have been honest," I said to him. "This looks horrible for you."

"But I didn't kill her," Edwin said. "She was alive when I left her. I wish I had proof for you, but ... I'll submit to DNA testing. Heck, measure my hands against the prints found around her neck if that's possible. I swear to every star in the sky that I would never hurt one of the girls. If anything, you need to look at *him*."

"I was planning to marry her," Carl said. "We were going to win this competition and then she was going to announce her retirement. We were thinking a tropical island for a few years. Get away from the craziness of this life for a while. Between the two of us, we had plenty of money to live off of for some time."

"Wait." I held up a hand. "I have one more suspect."

Both men looked for me to explain. I filled them in on Darren, the vendor, who still had a motive and opportunity to have silenced Mary for good. I explained about my race to the ferry and his subsequent ditch to the mainland, though I glossed over the fact that he was currently experiencing a deep emotional commitment to his hotel pillow.

"That's impossible," Carl said when I finished my story. "I was talking to Darren all morning."

"But —."

"While I was waiting at Coconuts for Mary to show up and play the keyboard, he stumbled in all out of sorts. He was running late to set his table up and thought they might have served coffee."

"I thought Darren was at the cottage that morning," I said. "He said he must have just missed the murderer."

"He was with me until eight fifteen," Carl said. "Like I said, he was already running late. But he recognized me and apologized for the face cream that'd made Mary break out in a rash. I told him it wasn't a huge deal. I even offered to help fine tune the product as a consultant if he wanted."

"So you and Mary weren't on bad terms with Darren?" I asked. "Neither of you were planning to ruin his career?"

"Of course not!" Carl recoiled, looking mortified. "I wouldn't do that and neither would Mary. She was the sweetest thing, and neither of us cared about anything except winning this stupid pageant and getting out of Dodge. We were planning to elope and retire from the business altogether — neither of us cared about some beauty product."

"I knew it." The soft, silky voice came from a third party — a shadowy figure that had managed to stay hidden in the darkness deeper in the alley. As the man spoke, he moved from behind a large Dumpster that'd hidden him from view. "I knew you were leaving me!"

"John?" Carl spun on his heel and stared at his assistant. "You don't know what we're talking about. What are you doing here, anyway? You said you didn't want to come tonight."

"I didn't *want* to be here," John said, moving under the

thin glow of a nearby streetlamp. He wore jeans and a plain black T-shirt, which gave him a distinctly more relaxed look than his butler's attire. "But I was forced to put a few things to rest."

At that, he raised a hand to reveal the metal glint of a gun.

"John, what is this about?" Carl raised his hands slightly as he stepped toward his assistant. "Put that gun away. This doesn't involve you."

"It does involve me. That's the problem, Carl, you didn't think about *me*. You haven't in a while, not since your wife left and Marilyn turned her stupid blue eyes on you."

"Marilyn — what?" Carl shook his head, not following as quickly as necessary. "I don't understand. Did you have something to do with Mary's death?"

"Everything to do with it." John hissed, stepping closer. "And now I'll have to finish it all in what will be the most awful murder spree in the history of Eternal Springs. Tragic, don't you think? All this beauty shrouded in ugliness."

"It doesn't have to be," I said, eyeing the gun warily. Though I was a witch, my skin most certainly didn't repel bullets. "Put the gun down. Nobody's seen you but us, and we don't have to say anything. You'll be okay, John."

"Someone's gonna turn me over to the cops." He winced. "And I don't look good in orange, so I'd prefer to shoot you."

"You're not a killer," I said. Carl seemed to have lost all capacity to speak. "Admit Marilyn's death was an accident. You'll get a lighter sentence. We'll vouch for you."

I was babbling and didn't mean a word that came out of my mouth, but I didn't know what else to do. There was a gun pointed at me, and I was flanked by two men paralyzed into speechlessness. I'd do just about anything to keep him busy and prevent the gun from firing at my chest.

"That's a load of crock and you know it," John spat. "The second I let you walk away from here you're going straight to those no-good cops. If it weren't for you, Evian, those cops would still be picking their noses with no clue that Mary's death was anything but an accident."

"Wasn't it an accident?" I coaxed. "Listen to me, John. I'm trying to help you. It *looked* like an accident — even the ME said so. There's no reason you can't claim that the two of you argued, things got out of hand and you panicked."

"Shut up," he said. "I'm sick of you. Stand against the wall, all three of you."

I gave Carl a glance, but he couldn't turn his eyes away from John. Resting a hand on the coach's shoulder, I gently guided his back against the wall and stood next to him. Edwin came to stand at my other shoulder.

"I told you I didn't kill her," Edwin said, surprisingly relaxed. He lit a new cigarette and took a pull. "But *no*, you wouldn't believe me."

"Is now the time?" I muttered. "We've got a psycho pointing a gun at us."

"He's not angry with me." Edwin shrugged. "You're the nosy person who couldn't leave this case alone."

"She shouldn't have left it alone!" Carl burst, finally snapping back to reality. "Mary is dead! She didn't deserve to die. John, how could you?"

Carl lunged toward John, who merely flinched and raised the gun.

I grasped Carl around the waist to hold him back and glared at Edwin. "A little help here?"

Edwin gave me a smirk then raised his cigarette and put it in front of Carl's face. "Step back, man. It's not worth it. One more step and you'll burn your eye out."

"Not exactly what I meant," I growled. "You could be less threatening. We're on the same team here."

"No, Edwin wasn't on the team," John said, straightening his shirt and resuming his stance after Carl's rush. "*We* were the dream team — me and Carl. Did Carl tell you he was training me as his coaching assistant? Together we were going to rule the world."

"Through beauty pageants?" Edwin frowned. "I stake my life on beauty pageants, and I don't think I'm taking over the world."

"If Marilyn had won that sixtieth pageant we could've gotten deals in any country. We would've coached girls from Milan to Paris to Rome to Budapest," he said. "But no, Carl gave up on the dream."

"Murdering Mary didn't help anything," I said. "Now, you're just two coaches with a dead client."

"She's not just a client!" Carl said. "She was my love."

"Pipe down, Carl," Edwin said, "or you'll get us all killed. You do that and your jerk-faced assistant walks free. You think the cops are onto him? *Nope*. So shut your pie hole and listen."

John gave a shudder and a nod. "I can't believe I'm agreeing with the worm, but he's right. Shut up."

"Why?" I asked quickly. We needed to keep him talking. "Why kill her?"

"The only way for us to succeed was for Mary to disappear."

"She could have quietly retired after winning," I said. "You sabotaged yourselves by silencing her."

"I am a *nobody*!" John shouted. "What don't you understand? Without Carl, there is no dream team. There's just *John*, which doesn't mean a thing. It needs to be John and Carl. If Mary stole Carl away to some stupid island, I would have been nothing. I would have been less than nothing — I wouldn't have a job, let alone an empire. Together, we could have made millions, traveled the world, created a legacy. But he threw it all away."

"What's the point of it all?" Carl asked, his eyes tearing up again despite the terror of being held at gunpoint. "What's the point of making money, creating a legacy, traveling the world, if you don't have someone by your side? If you don't have love?"

"You did have love, Carl!" John looked furious. "I have always been there for you. I was loyal to you. When your wife left, I was there. When you needed tampons for your clients in the middle of the night, who ran to buy them? When you found out Mary had died, who picked you up again?"

"You wouldn't have had to pick me up if you didn't kill her!" Carl snarled. "You are not loyal to me, you pig! That wasn't love — it was selfishness."

"What is love if not respect, patience, servitude? I was all those things to you for years! Then Mary comes along and I'm nothing but the assistant once again. I wasn't getting walked on all over again."

"You were never *just* my assistant," Carl said, his voice weak. "You were always my closest friend, confidant, supporter — and I was yours. Mary didn't change any of that. She only enhanced it."

"Not in the way I liked." John shifted uncomfortably.

In an odd way, I suspected that John truly did have some sort of love, or at least deep sense of loyalty and friendship to Carl. It was a shame that something once so positive had manifested in such a horrible way.

As John explained how Mary had ruined everything, I let my eyes flick shut for the briefest of moments. An idea floated into my head, put there by some little bit of magic. Tonight was a full moon, and under the full moon I had special talents. Nothing that would take down a psychotic killer with a flick of my finger, but I might be able to pull off something that would throw off his game enough to escape being shot.

"*Sprinkle water by the new full moon,*" I murmured, splitting my attention between the precipitation in the nearby clouds and the man before us. "*Then watch your garden grow and bloom!*"

"What'd you say?" John asked. "What did you — ah, *no*. You've got to be kidding me! *What* is this?"

As the first drops of rain fell isolated on John, I glanced at the men next to me and shouted, "Move!"

I raised my hands and concentrated harder, bringing the rain down with a vicious pelting motion that pummeled my target with hail-like drops. I disguised the movements of my hands as I leapt toward him, and Carl followed suit. I lost track of Edwin in the scuffle.

"Drop the weapon," I shouted, but John didn't listen. "Drop it *now!*"

John raised his hands to defend himself against the onslaught of rain blurring his vision and struck out with a kick. His foot flew at my face, and on pure reaction I swung out and gave his leg an extra shove.

"You monster!" Carl landed the second blow straight to John's gut with a full-on football tackle.

The two men tumbled to the ground, the gun clattering into the darkness down the alley. I chased after it, gave it another firm kick with my stiletto so it was completely masked by weeds and darkness, and then returned to help Carl.

John had gotten in a few punches that had left Carl's lip bloodied and his nose smeared red. The latter's eye was already blackening. Carl wouldn't be winning any beauty contests in the near future.

I sized up the rolling duo and struck at my first opportunity. John rolled to his back and stared into the sky while Carl flopped onto his chest and pinned the murderer to the ground. I neatly pressed the heel of my stiletto against his private parts and smiled down at John.

"Make one more move," I said, "and the stiletto goes straight through your manhood."

I couldn't be sure if Mason had rounded the corner in time to hear me deliver that line, but later he assured me that yes, he'd heard every last word of my terrifying threat. No wonder I could never hold onto a boyfriend.

The cops rounded the corner shortly after, and before I knew it, John was in handcuffs and babbling a full confession. Edwin returned to his cigarette, Carl collapsed into a fit of despair, and Mason very carefully avoided any mention of my stilettos.

H appily ever ... *almost*.

Twenty-Four

"I'm so sorry," Mason said, for what must have been the twentieth time later that evening. "I am so sorry. I couldn't leave Billie Jo's side with all the funny stuff going on at the bar. Kenna finally came down and took her off my hands so I could look for you. I wouldn't have let you go alone had I known ... ."

"Mason." I smiled and cut him off with a wave of my hand. "None of this is your fault. I just appreciate you showing up when you did and calling the police."

"The police," he said, his voice grim. "They should've been involved much sooner so you — a *civilian* — didn't have to go through this. John had a gun, Evian. Pointed at *you*."

And I had the full moon and some pretty nifty water powers, I thought to myself, but I said: "And I had some sweet shoes, don't you think?"

I held up my stilettos. The shoes might be both beautiful and deadly, that was for certain. And well worth every penny. Mason gave a shudder. "Don't remind me."

I laughed. "I'm going to head home for tonight, okay?"

"Let me walk you back. It's the least I can do. Are you

sure you don't want to stay over at my place? Not in any sort of romantic way," he added quickly, "purely for safety."

I winked. "Nice line, but no thank you. And I will be fine. My friends are coming with me. Right, ladies?"

Skye, Kenna and Zola nodded. I'd promised Skye an exclusive interview, Zola an extra dose of magical water on her plants, and Kenna ... well, I'd promised to sing a solo during the karaoke night. The catch for all those favors, of course, was for a little help in getting Bob back to where he belonged.

"It's been a long night," Kenna said, gesturing outside. "It's almost morning."

With a shudder, I looked outside and realized that was true. My powers would only remain at maximum strength for another hour or two. We needed to move now or else banishing Bob would be all but impossible.

In many ways the night had been a success. Kenna had gotten a ridiculously crazy turnout at her event and the beauty pageant was sure to draw an even bigger crowd of tourists than expected. Skye would have her inside scoop and Zola would have her crops specially dosed with my water charm. And I'd finally agreed to Mason's offer of a dinner date.

"I'll see you tomorrow, okay?" I told the mechanic. "I have the day off. If you grab a coffee around ten, we just might run into each other."

He leaned in and gave me a kiss on the cheek. "Have a nice night, Evian. Don't go looking for trouble."

"Who *me*?" I asked with a light laugh. "I don't look for it. Usually. It just seems to find me."

He gave a confused sort of grin, and then began the trudge up the hill toward home. Halfway up, he turned for one last wave.

"He's got it bad for you," Zola said with a snicker. "Super cute."

I fought back a blush. "The sun will be up shortly. Shall we?"

After ensuring we weren't followed by any gossip mongers looking for an even bigger scoop, we slipped onto the path behind my house. Bertha was fast asleep, judging by the snores that radiated across the fields from her open bedroom window. She liked the breeze.

Our walk up and over the fields behind my house passed quickly. There wasn't a sound, save for the murmured curses from Skye at getting her feet dirty. All was quiet under the last fingers of the full moon's reach.

"What's our plan when we find Bob?" I asked. "Any thoughts?"

"He's *your* problem," Skye said. "We're just with you for backup."

"I don't love that rule about whomever sees him banishes him," I said. "You're not really going to make me do this alone, are you?"

Kenna shrugged. "You were just fine with the rule when it was us banishing monsters."

I groaned, but she had a point. "Fine, I'll do it. But if I get in trouble, send some fireballs his way or something."

"We'll see," Kenna said primly. "If you get rid of him yourself, we won't even have to go there."

Skye pointed down toward a giant blob in the distance: "Is that tub of lard the thing you're afraid of?"

I peeked out from behind the bushes and spotted Bob. His body had expanded both in length and in rotundity since I'd last seen him. He was absolutely, positively, the biggest monster I'd ever seen.

"That's Bob," I said.

"He doesn't look so bad." Zola frowned, studying him. "If anything, he looks pretty blissful to me."

Indeed, Bob appeared to be languidly munching the flowers that Zola and I had planted and watered. Our plan had worked. Bob sat just feet from the portal that'd send him back to where he'd come from — and all I needed to do was get him over the tipping point.

"Last chance for any of you to take all the glory," I said, rolling up my sleeves. "Going once, going twice ... ."

"Sold to the water witch." Kenna clapped me on the back. "We'll watch from here. Holler if you need help."

"Might be too late if he bites my head off first!" I hissed to her as I inched out, leaving my stilettos behind. Thankfully the portal was surrounded by patches of grass soft enough to tickle the soles of my feet. "All right, Bob. It's me and you."

The slug sat in a patch of moonlight just starting to burn off into morning. There was no way my size would help in this battle, so I opted to use the same technique I'd employed against John. My sparkling cleverness ... *yeah*, right.

"Come on, big guy," I said, closing my eyes and drawing in water with the last of the full moon's energy as I prepared my charm. "Help me out. Go on home, will you buddy?"

I inched a raincloud closer and closer, drawing it near with a nifty little spell that'd been passed down from previous water witches. The coven would be proud, I thought, if only the members could be bothered to hop over to Eternal Springs once in a blue moon. It wasn't a simple thing to move an entire cloud.

"Get him," Skye said. "What are you waiting for! The sun's coming up."

"Is he changing color?" Kenna asked. "What the heck is up with his skin?"

Bob's purple coloring faded to a dullish, metallic gray, and

I knew before I took my next breath that the worst had happened: Bob had become an adult.

A tiny voice croaked through the night air. *Do it now!*

"Paul?" I glanced up just in time to see my familiar taking a flying leap through the air. "What are you doing here?"

I'm helping you! No supernatural slug will kill my witch! Paul landed on the top of Bob's head, where he stuck with a slight suction sound. *I'll get his eyes, you send the rain into the portal — he'll follow his nose*

"But Paul —."

No time to talk, he said as Bob's head turned toward me and a hungry gleam appeared in his eyes. *If you die, who will make my margaritas just the way I like them?*

"You're so thoughtful," I grunted, as Bob lunged my way. I dove, holding my hands out and taking the brunt of the fall with my shoulder as I rolled out of the way.

Send rain into the portal — he'll follow the water!

I did as Paul suggested. I unleashed every drop of precipitation from the storm cloud hovering over the island, screaming the incantation as I poured charmed water into the portal. Zola rushed forward as well, raising her hands as she sent several flowers hurtling through the opening. Together, it was enough.

Paul bounced between the slug's eyes to seal the deal. When Bob lost his sight, he staggered drunkenly, nearly crushing me beneath him. I dove toward Zola and pulled her toward the woods as Bob took one giant sniff of the air, caught a whiff of the magical water and enchanted plants, and dove into the portal.

Paul went with him.

I scurried to my feet, rushed over and crumpled to the ground. "Paul! Come back!"

There was a long silence as I stared after my beloved familiar. He'd toppled over the edge along with Bob. I couldn't handle the shock of being separated from Paul. We'd been connected far too long to imagine life without him.

"Oh, Paul, you can have all the margaritas you want," I said. "I'll buy you a new bed and let you sleep in the den. Just come back, Paul."

A croak, and then one little reptilian foot planted itself on the edge of the portal. *I'm gonna hold you to that.*

"Oh, Paul, thank goodness!" I scooped my toad out of the portal, sent a hex downward to seal it temporarily closed, and then deposited Paul on my shoulder. "Jeesh, you didn't have to scare me like that."

Do I make for a good hero or what? How about getting me a cape?

"Let's not push it."

Twenty-Five

"What a night, huh?" I plopped into a beanbag chair I'd situated on the porch next to Paul's bed. "You were something out there, let me tell you."

You weren't so bad yourself. Say, for breakfast, how about some mimosas to celebrate?

"You're going to milk your heroism for all its worth, aren't you?"

Yep.

I heaved myself back to my feet and returned to the kitchen. Paul and I had slept in late. After banishing Bob back to the correct realm last night, I had followed Zola back to her gardens and bewitched a watering can. It allowed her to water any plant she wanted so long as the full moon reflected off its surface. It had returned to its status as a regular old watering can as of this morning.

We'd snuck back in before Bertha woke this morning, so there were no explanations needed about our late-night gallivanting through the woods. Four women out after dark walking barefoot under a full moon? Her suspicions would have been on high alert. Every now and then I suspected she knew there was more to our story than the nun cover, but I'd never know. It wasn't as though I could confirm our witchiness to her even if she guessed.

I returned to the porch with one mimosa for Paul and a steaming mug of coffee for me. I'd just plunked Paul's cup on the floor when a voice called my name from the street.

"Hey, Evian. I think this belongs to you."

Straightening, I peered out front to a most wonderful sight. My gorgeous scooter was parked at the side of the street. The man standing next to it wasn't all that bad looking either. Mason smiled at my surprised expression and gave a wave that said to come down and take a look.

"Wow, it looks perfect!" I said, letting my free hand smooth over the seat while I gripped my coffee tight in the other hand. "Does it run?"

"What sort of mechanic would I be if I returned a Vespa that didn't run?" He crossed his arms across a broad chest. "Of course it runs. Feel free to take it for a test drive."

"I trust you," I said on instinct, but the second the words were out of my mouth I knew them to be true. "I mean ... I'm sorry, Mason. About the whole suspicion of you for murder. I never *really* thought it was you, but I had to keep a clear head. I hope you can understand."

"Just so long as you show up for our date tomorrow, all is forgiven."

He grinned broader, looking a bit like a cowboy with his tired jeans and threadbare T-shirt. But in a good way. He looked fresh under the morning sun, and his smile was pleasant and warmed me more than the coffee.

"Oh," he added, a quick frown monopolizing his features. "I thought you should know — John's locked up, obviously, for the murder of Mary — no bail."

"Poor Mary. Poor Carl, too," I said. "Do you know how he's holding up?"

"He's going to stay to see the pageant through. Once it's done he's heading out to that island anyway for a few weeks' break. Turns out Edwin stepped down voluntarily from his position, too. Not into the beauty scene anymore, he claims."

"Well, thanks for the update," I said, and then gestured awkwardly to the bike. "And thanks for this. Let me grab my checkbook."

"Later," he said and winked. "I know where to find you. In fact, are you free right now? I was heading to the café and was hoping I could buy you a latte."

I glanced at my coffee mug, then up at his hopeful expression.

I dumped my mug at the edge of my garden. "I'd love to get coffee with you, Mason. Let me grab a sweatshirt."

Mason nodded, leaning against the fence as I jogged onto the porch and grabbed my sweatshirt from the hook. I bent over, pretending to tie my shoes, and gave a quick whispered update to Paul.

I heard everything. I'm your freaking familiar.

"See you, then," I said. "Don't go looking for trouble."

On my way back to Mason I caught sight of something that made me halt halfway to the street.

"Look at this! Mason, it's a flower!"

"Sure," he said, seemingly unimpressed. "That's ... great?"

I glanced around my yard, the former mud pits, and realized they'd already hardened. In a sure sign of new beginnings, I noticed a few little sprouts had begun to poke through the blanket of black to spot my yard with green. Apparently evicting Bob had been just the ticket to recovering my lawn. Even Bertha's raspberries seemed plumper than ever, though I dared not pick one for fear she'd put it on my bill.

I stood, whistling at the sight of the perfect little daisy next to my sneakers. The warmth of the sun was on my face, I had a coffee date with a mechanic and my toad had saved the day.

Some might call that good fortune. Others might call it luck.

I happened to think it might just be ... *magic*.

Author's Note

Thank you for reading! I hope you enjoyed meeting Evian Brooks, along with her friends, Kenna, Skye, and Zola. It was an absolute joy to work with Amanda, Leighann, and Annabel on this shared world project—so be sure to go back and pick up the first three books in the series if you haven't yet! To be notified of other new releases, please sign up for my newsletter at www.ginalamanna.com.

Thanks again for reading!
Gina

Also by Gina LaManna

Gina LaManna is the USA TODAY bestselling author of the Magic & Mixology series, the Lacey Luzzi Mafia Mysteries, The Little Things romantic suspense series, and the Misty Newman books.

The Hex Files:

Wicked Never Sleeps

Wicked Long Nights

Lola Pink Mystery Series:

Shades of Pink

Shades of Stars

Shades of Sunshine

Magic & Mixology Mysteries:

Hex on the Beach

Witchy Sour

Jinx & Tonic

Long Isle Iced Tea

Amuletto Kiss

MAGIC, Inc. Mysteries:

The Undercover Witch

Reading Order for Lacey Luzzi:

Lacey Luzzi: Scooped

Lacey Luzzi: Sprinkled

Lacey Luzzi: Sparkled

Lacey Luzzi: Salted

Lacey Luzzi: Sauced

Lacey Luzzi: S'mored

Lacey Luzzi: Spooked

Lacey Luzzi: Seasoned

Lacey Luzzi: Spiced

Lacey Luzzi: Suckered

Lacey Luzzi: Sugared

Lacey Luzzi: Sprouted

The Little Things Mystery Series:

One Little Wish

Two Little Lies

Misty Newman:

Teased to Death

Short Story in Killer Beach Reads

Chick Lit:

Girl Tripping

Gina also writes books for kids under the Pen Name Libby LaManna:

Mini Pie the Spy!

Made in the USA
Monee, IL
25 November 2022